CW00517144

The Tell-Fang Heart

Vampire Pet Boutique Mysteries No. 2

Elle Wren Burke

Copyright © 2023 by Elle Wren Burke

All rights reserved.

No portion of this book may be reproduced in any form without written permission from the publisher or author, except as permitted by U.S. copyright law.

Cover design by Mariah Sinclair

Contents

Chapter One

"Look at this smooshie face! Who has a smooshie face? You do!"

Thwack thwack thwack

"Yes, you're a good boy! Such a good boy!"

Thwack thwack thwack thwack thwack

A chocolate-brown tail attached to an adorable pitbull banged against a display of hand-woven cat beds made by a lovely local vampire.

Despite a frenzy of customers around us, I only had eyes for him. "Do you want a treat, Xander?"

Thwack thwack thwack thwack thwack thwack thwack

"Okay, let's get one!"

Xander was a big fan of our pinwheel-shaped peanut-butter dog treats. When they visited my pet boutique, Matilda's VamPets, his owner always let me give him one. Or two. I turned my chair to grab one from the pink treat bar behind me, maneuvering my wheelchair deftly and confidently. I knew every inch of the store and when and how fast to take turns in my pet boutique.

CRASH

Or so I thought.

Absorbed in my gush session with Xander—who is named after *that* Xander from *Buffy*, in case you were wondering—I hadn't noticed that his rather thick tail had moved the clear plastic display several inches.

The display teetered onto one edge, but fortunately, before it could totter, Xander's owner, Billy, launched toward it with his vampire speed and caught it.

Unfortunately, though, Billy isn't the most coordinated vampire on the planet, so in his haste, he knocked into one of my five-foot-tall white wood shelves, causing three bottles of lavender dog perfume to hit the painted-concrete floor.

Xander was apparently not a fan of crashing glass, so he tried to jump into my lap, which went as well as you would think an eighty-pound dog launching itself at a wheelchair would go.

Not well—especially considering that my brakes weren't set.

The chair rolled straight back into the treat bar with a *thump*. Xander somehow managed to keep his front legs on my thighs, which was *great* for my chronic pain.

All my customers froze, staring. A young vamp even had one hand over her heart and the other over her mouth, her comically big eyes fixated on the shattered bottles.

Holding up the unbreakable cat beds, Billy took in the broken glass and my new pitbull-shaped lap ornament. His face rapidly changed from surprise to horror to embarrassment.

"Oh my stars, Josie!" He righted the cat beds and rushed to my side. "Are you okay? I should have just let the cat beds fall. I'm so sorry about the bottles! And I'm so sorry Xander jumped on you."

"It's okay, though maybe you could get him down now?"

Billy gently pulled Xander to the ground, being careful to lead him away from the broken glass.

Running a hand over his buzz cut, he pleaded with me, "Let me pay you for the perfumes. And do you have a broom? I'll clean it up!"

"Don't worry about it, Billy. It's just part of doing business. We'll clean it up, and you don't need to pay for it. You're a loyal customer. It'll pay for itself."

Right on time, my employee Lacey rushed up with a broom and cleaning supplies. The crowd that'd formed around us dispersed as they realized the drama was over.

"Oh no, please let me pay," Billy insisted.

After about five more minutes of begging, I waved my arms to cut him off. "Billy, I run a *pet boutique*. Animals of all sizes come in here, and some of these fancy items are bound to break. It's fine." I held my hand up as he tried to protest. "Seriously. It's fine."

He finally nodded, acquiescing.

"Now, let's get Xander that treat." I turned in my chair to grab two pinwheels. "Okay, Xander, sit!" His butt hit the floor instantly. "Down!" His chest hit the floor too. "Roll over!" Nothing. "Roll over!" Xander let out a little whine. "Still not understanding that trick, huh? Let's try...up!" He shot straight from ground to air in one nimble movement. "Good job!" I finally handed him the treats.

Billy took Xander to the front of the store and grabbed a shopping basket—pink, of course, like the accents in the store and on my wheelchair. In his determination to make up for the perfume, he started adding everything in sight to it—including a calming spray for cats that he certainly didn't need. He was allergic.

Laughing under my breath, I thanked Lacey and did a lap around the store. As I passed the wall across from the treat bar, a tiny meow caught my attention. Atop a weathered white table sat a two-tiered cat kennel. It would have been fine on the floor, but I wanted to elevate it away from any doggy mouths.

"Hey there, Reginald. How are you today, buddy?"

The long-haired cream-colored cat let out another meow and rubbed against the side of his cage, his red-and-pink striped bow tie grazing the wire frame.

It was almost Valentine's Day, and I was hoping the love in the air would help Reginald get adopted. Our local animal shelter had approached me recently about working together.

Help an adoptable cat that I could snuggle with in my downtime? Umm, yes, please. It was a no-brainer. We'd set everything up, and Reginald had moved in a few days ago.

To give him his best chance, I'd put him in the adorable bow tie, and covered the outside of his kennel with red and pink hearts, just like the rest of my store.

Hearts hung from the ceiling. Heart-shaped string lights stretched across the walls. Displays of toys shaped like conversation hearts with sayings like "BE MINE" and "BITE ME" were scattered throughout the store. Valentine's Day cat and dog sweaters and bandannas hung on the wall.

"Aww, I know. You want attention. I'd take you into my office, but we're pretty busy right now."

I stuck my finger between the wires, not at all worried that gentle Reginald would bite me.

A young human-vampire couple noticed us and immediately started fawning all over Reggie.

I let them be and continued my loop. Lacey had finished cleaning and was restocking the conversation hearts. All the browsing customers looked fine, but a line was forming at the back counter.

My store manager and cousin, Dawk, looked harried. His flannel shirt had come untucked and his light-blond hair, an exact match for my own shade, was bursting from his head in all directions.

I wheeled behind the counter to see what was causing my cousin so much distress and to lend a hand. The low white sales counter, installed just a few months ago after I got my wheelchair, was the perfect height for me to roll under. I checked for my Scottish Terrier and store namesake, Matilda, as I got myself in position. She usually liked to sleep under the counter, but all the activity must have caused her to flee to the quiet storeroom.

I set my brakes and listened in.

"But when you say 'Cupid-shaped cake,' how detailed is it? Will I be able to see every little curl on Cupid's head?" The gorgeous vampire—whose hair was pulled so tightly into a low bun that I swear her skin was stretching—waved an arm through the air in a curlicue motion. "Will I be able to see the details of his bow and arrow? And are you absolutely sure all the ingredients are dog-safe?"

Dawk looked at me, the exasperation clear on his face. I gave him a big, exaggerated smile and slid the laminated paper with the example cakes on it across the counter to him.

Grabbing it, he said to Tight-Bun, "Yes, as I mentioned, these ingredients are used in the normal dog cakes we sell. The baker, Isa," he gestured to the left where Isa's bakery was located next door, "is a seasoned baker of dog confections. Everything is safe." He held the laminated sheet up. "These are the example cakes. As you can see, the mold has a bit of definition around the hair and bow and arrow."

She wrinkled her nose and proceeded to ask three hundred more questions.

Our store normally offered bone and heart-shaped cakes for dogs. We took the orders and passed them to Isa. She took a larger share of the proceeds from the cakes, while I got the benefit of extra business. Usually ordered for canine birthdays or gotcha days, people loved to buy extra goodies to go with the cakes, like birthday hats. It was a win-win for us both.

I'd had the idea about six weeks before to do a Valentine's Day promotion. The heart-shaped cakes we already offered were perfect, but I thought it would be fun to offer Cupid-shaped cakes using a mold I found online. We were charging more for those, as they'd require more detailed icing work, but we were also charging extra for the limited-edition factor.

I'd done a major marketing push for the promotion, touting it in the town's private Facebook group, on VampTube, and on flyers we'd hung in both the boutique and the bakery. Our friend Bayla owned the town's blood and wine bar and she'd agreed to take a stack of flyers as well.

My efforts had paid off. We'd been taking orders for the last few weeks. As we got closer to today, the last day to order, more and more dog owners were coming in. It seemed like every dog in Arteria Falls was going to have a heart or Cupid cake.

Leaving Dawk to handle Tight-Bun, I rolled to the register and called out, "I can help the next customer!"

Dawk shot me a jealous look as I took the next person's cake order in under a minute. They were also buying an adorable bandanna that said, "Cuter than Cupid."

I called out for the next customer while Dawk was reassuring Tight-Bun for the tenth time that the cakes were safe for dogs. A man with blond hair just a shade darker than mine and Dawk's—and wearing a yellow polo that clashed with it horribly—approached the counter with a big smile.

"Busy in here today, huh?"

I smiled back. "Yep! We've got a big Valentine's Day promotion going. I see you have some cat toys. How many cats do you have?"

"Just the one cat. A recent addition to my household."

"Well, that explains why I haven't seen you in here before!" I said cheerily. "Oh, you have one of our Valentine's bow ties too. How fun."

The man nodded. "When I saw it on the kitty up front, I knew I needed one for my Sally."

"Sally. What a cute name." I scanned the man's items, and he tapped his credit card to pay. As I was handing him the pink plastic bag full of his purchases, something about his face caught my eye. "You look familiar."

"You do too." He gave me a searching look. "I've got it—Fun for Fangs!"

A light blinked on in my head. "You're right! We sorted toys together. That must have been, what, six years ago?"

He rubbed his hand over a light layer of blond stubble on his chin. "Yeah, I think six years. I haven't seen you there since."

I winced. Fun for Fangs was our vampire version of Toys for Tots. I'd had to stop volunteering there in recent years. It was just too much for my body on top of my daily life.

Noticing my wince, the man kindly changed the topic. "Well, you've done well with your cake promotion. This is quite the crowd. Have a great Valentine's Day!"

And with that, I moved on to the next customer.

Poor Dawk was still talking to Tight-Bun.

Chapter Two

"Isa! How are you, my lovely friend?"

I stopped at the edge of the counter in Isa's Eats. The day's rush was well over, and the bakery was closing soon. Isa's shop assistant, Hadley, was helping their last few customers. Isa stood at the far side of the counter scribbling in a binder, lost in her task.

Careful not to get in Hadley's way, I flipped my brakes back and rolled to Isa's side. "Isa!" Nothing.

Seeing as I was level with her belly button, clearly the only option to get her attention was to poke it with a dark-red fingernail.

"ARRRGH!" Isa shouted, her curly ponytail bouncing as she jumped back. "Josie! What the fangs?"

Laughing all the way down to my belly, I reached out to grab her forearm. "Sorry, not sorry. That was the best part of my day so far."

"Mmm hmm," she said, giving me the stink eye. She eased her arm away from me and asked, "What can I help you with, Jos?"

"I just emailed you another set of orders. People are loving the Cupid cakes, but a decent amount of folks are ordering the cheaper hearts. We've already taken over twenty orders today. At least we're closing in an hour, so hopefully, we won't get many more."

The baker groaned. "*Twenty?* Thank the stars I ordered a massive amount of ingredients. I don't know how I'm going to make all these orders, though. I'll have to start as soon as we close on the thirteenth. Hadley is going to help but…"

"Yes?" I waved my arm, inviting her to continue.

"But I think I need more help. There's no time to hire someone. So I'll need to call in reinforcements."

I nodded, understanding her meaning. "Gotcha. Let me think." I counted off on my fingertips. "Dawk, Disha, Lynnae, Calder, and Elm will all help."

She raised an eyebrow at me. "You sound quite sure about that considering you haven't asked them yet."

I bared my fangs. "Don't worry, I'll make them help. You just worry about all the prep. Today's the ninth, so there are still several days for us to work out the details."

She gave me a quick nod, but her brow was still tight with concern.

I rubbed her back. "It will all work out. They're all prepaid, so as long as we give them something that resembles cake with a spattering of icing, we're good. No refunds!"

Her eyes widened, and her body tensed. Before she popped a blood vessel, I held my hands out, "Kidding! Of course each cake will look fanging amazing."

Before I could give her another heart attack, she shooed me out of her bakery.

Seeing Isa always boosted my mood, so I left for my shop with a smile on my face. Brisk air met me as the door opened. I hadn't bothered to throw my coat over my boxy magenta sweater, so I pushed hard on my handrims as I rolled onto Vein Street's brick sidewalk.

It was an easy journey now that Isa and I had both upgraded our doors. She wanted her shop to be accessible too, so we'd sought out the perfect doors—glass with long, vertical handles that could be reached from most heights and handicap access switches that swung the doors inward when pushed. We'd also added threshold ramps to make rolling in and out painless.

As I approached my shop, I noticed a new edition on the door. A red heart the size of my palm cut perfectly from construction paper. The hearts I'd decorated with were made of foil, so someone else must have left it for us.

"Aww, we have a Valentine's Fairy Godmother, or maybe a *Fangy* Godmother."

Chuckling at my horrible joke, I pushed the access button and rolled inside.

Chapter Three

The evening air was crisp against my skin as I climbed out of my van. That's right—I'd bought a van.

I'd tried squeezing my wheelchair into all my friend's vehicles before concluding that I needed something roomier. The van was perfect.

Blood red with a tan interior, it had all kinds of fun gadgets and technology, but most importantly, I was able to remove a seat from the middle row. Zippy, as I'd named my wheelchair, fit perfectly in the empty space behind the driver's seat.

I slid open the middle door and took a deep breath. Getting Zippy out of the van was a bit precarious. I had to grab the arms in just the right spot while making sure I kept my back as relaxed as possible. While the wheelchair was a lightweight model, it was still upward of twenty pounds—enough to have given me several back spasms over the last few months.

Once I was ready, I lifted Zippy and backed up several steps. Making sure to bend only as far as needed, I set the chair down.

I twisted to the side an inch or two, checking if my back was okay. "Another successful chair removal, Matilda!"

My little Scottie wagged at me from the remaining middle-row chair.

I sat down and rolled the chair out of her way. "Okay, girl! You can come out now."

It had taken weeks, but I'd successfully trained her to wait in her seat until I told her otherwise. Being the very good girl she was, she now waited patiently no matter where we were.

Not bothering to pick up her leash, I let her bounce to the front porch of our bungalow, where she started sniffing the plants my roommate, Lynnae, kept there. The porch held an array of plants during the warmer months, but those were now crowding the inside of my bungalow, practically every surface holding a plant. Now that it was winter, Lynnae had placed a few potted blue spruces and boxwoods around the rocking chairs on the porch.

Matilda was quite possessive of the porch and had to make certain no other animals had invaded her territory. Those were her plants, as far as she was concerned.

I closed the van door and followed her to the porch. Luckily, we had a walkway from our driveway to the porch that was easy to roll on, and the porch was accessible with just a tiny ramp.

After pushing open the oak front door, I took a deep breath, really drawing the cold Colorado air into my lungs. "Home sweet home, Matilda. Let's go inside."

A few minutes later, Matilda and I were curled up on the couch. I'd tucked us under an emerald-green knit blanket that matched my velvet couch perfectly. I pushed my favorite golden-yellow pillow behind my back and let my body relax.

But I was still too cold. Chronic pain and cold are not friends. They're staunch enemies, battling constantly, but the cold always wins.

I threw a navy-blue fleece blanket over us too. "Matilda, the temperature has dropped twenty degrees since this afternoon." I grabbed my phone from the coffee table and opened my thermostat app. "Let's turn the heat up."

I switched out my phone for a blood bag I'd grabbed from the fridge. Nothing special, just O− with a little bit of chocolate mixed in.

Once I drained the bag, I picked up the glossy green journal I'd taken to leaving on the coffee table. Lynnae had texted that she was—surprise, surprise—working late, so I took the time to myself to get some insightful journaling done.

Just kidding. I'd tried to journal in the past, but I'd just end up staring at the pages blankly, feeling like a loser. Did I really have nothing to say about my own life?

No, this little green book was for something else.

I ran my fingers around the rim with a sigh. Matilda raised her head to check on me. "I'm okay, girl. Just...stuck."

Opening the journal, I let my fingers slowly flip through the thick, cream pages. Activity logs. Known contacts. Recent cases. Potential enemies.

Everything my grandfather had done, everyone he'd talked to, everything he'd worked on, everyone who'd hated him leading up to his disappearance a few years ago.

Obsession was a mild way to describe my previous addiction to my Grandpa Roan's vanishing. It had been my whole world, my whole purpose. I'd eventually ended my search for him after my family and friends had begged me to stop. It was killing me, they'd said. They'd been right.

But I hadn't been able to bring myself to get rid of my files. This journal, several boxes worth of evidence, files from the cases we'd worked together in his PI business, a cork board in my closet I'd dubbed The Vanishing Wall.

Thank the Goddess, I still had it all. And a few new things too. Back in October, I'd received two cryptic notes. I'd blown the first one off, but when I got the second alongside a pair of excised fangs, I could feel in my blood vessels that the sender had information about my grandfather.

The notes seemed to be telling me that the sender knew where my grandfather was, that he had information the sender wanted, and that I could find this information too. The notes heavily implied that there'd be consequences not just for us, but all vamps, if I didn't find it.

But I had no idea what it was the sender wanted me to find.

They'd given me no indication as to what I should be looking for.

Grandpa Roan knew a lot of things—which thing was it? And why was it so important? Had he disappeared to protect the information? If so, I should let it be. Or maybe he'd left to find this information. But if that was the case, how would I find it here?

With a frustrated grunt, I threw the book down. Nothing in there would help me. I'd been over it a thousand times.

No, I needed to move on from guessing at what the information could be.

I needed a new tactic, and thankfully, the sender themselves had given me one.

Finding them.

The sender was the only concrete link I had, so if I could find them, maybe I could find my Grandpa Roan. But they were elusive. I'd interviewed all my neighbors. No one had seen anything the days the notes were left.

I'd checked my doorbell camera. No one had approached the house the entirety of the first day I'd received a note. The second day was trickier, as we'd had a big party, but I combed the footage over and over until I was convinced our guests had been the only ones on it. My neighbor across the street has a doorbell camera too, but he'd told me he didn't actually keep the footage because he wasn't "a paranoid numskull" but just wanted to know when his "mollycoddling" son was at the door so he could pretend to be asleep.

The sender had gotten around the camera somehow, so I'd had to get more creative.

Leaning forward, I grabbed two bulging file folders and a highlighter off the coffee table.

Flipping to a new page, I read,

Paddington, Emelyn 10/08/22 13:01

Paddington, Markus 10/08/22 13:01

Smith, Howie 10/08/22 13:15

VampEx #85746 Kelvin, Antony 10/08/22 13:20

VampEx #85788 Handler, Leonora 10/08/22 13:23

Kierney, Madison 10/08/22 13:45

None of the names rang a bell.

After his disappearance, I'd tried to convince the Office of Town Security to give me the entry logs for the last week Grandpa Roan was in town. They'd laughed in my face the first time, and by the twentieth time I'd asked, they'd banned me from their office.

I'd tried bribing some of the security officers, but they were all too afraid. The records were too locked down, too private to share, they'd said.

You see, you can't just walk into Arteria Falls. It is a hidden town, after all. All of our vampire towns are located in secluded areas. A land buffer exists around each town. Electric fences surround the land, and security cameras dot the fence posts.

Arteria Falls is a bit different, as it's built on the plains but right up against the Rocky Mountains. Fences line the mountain side of the border, but it's more difficult to protect. Officers have to patrol the area regularly, a duty they take very seriously.

Each citizen of the vampire world, vampire or human, has a little key fob containing an encrypted ID chip that grants them entry through each town's single access point. We all understand the need to keep records of who enters, but no one wants their movements made public, so those records are locked down tightly.

But I had new leverage I didn't have last time—a guard with a gambling problem. He'd managed to hide it from his superiors, but I'd spent many November nights following guards around, looking for something I could exploit.

I'd approached the guard in December, keeping things friendly at first, but by January, I'd revealed my hand and offered them a nice chunk of money for the records.

The records were even more important now, so I was more than willing to pay. Before, I had no idea what had happened to my grandfather, so the records might not have been helpful at all.

But now someone had left me the notes. My gut told me the sender wasn't local. Whatever this was about, it was bigger than me, bigger than Arteria Falls.

If the same person who left the notes also took my grandfather, I could cross-reference the logs. See if anyone had entered town before the disappearance and before the notes were left.

My guard contact came through a week ago, so I'd been spending every night sorting through the mountain of paper. In a spreadsheet, I would have been done in about five minutes, but digital files would have been way too risky for the guard, so I was stuck with paper records.

I hadn't found anything yet, except a few paper cuts, but I wasn't even close to done. Not even close.

Chapter Four

"Boss, I can't tell you how happy I am that we're done taking orders for the promotion. I almost lost it yesterday."

"Dawk, don't be silly. It's perfectly normal for the customers to ask you where every single ingredient in the cake is sourced from and whether they're fair trade."

My cousin ran his hands down his face, clearly reliving the moment. "I think that lady's hair was so tight that it was pulling on her brain. I hope she never comes back."

I rolled toward Reginald's kennel with a nice bowl of canned food and kibbles balanced on a wooden tray on my lap, leaving Dawk back at the sales counter. "You realize she still has to pick the cake up on Valentine's Day, right?"

"Fangs. I'm hiding in the back as soon as I see her."

I laughed. "Fair enough. If she starts asking me questions, I can always slowly roll back from her until the distance between us is so awkward that she's forced to leave."

"The advantages of a wheelchair!" Dawk said with a chuckle.

"Oh, there are so many advantages!" I said with only a hint of sarcasm. "For one, I'm level with.Mr. Reginald's kennel here too."

Reginald rubbed against the side of the kennel as he let out a long *meow*.

"Are you excited about your food?"

Meow

"Should I refill your water too?"

Meow

"Yes, I should. You've had a lot already this morning."

Meow

I opened the little door and exchanged his water bowl for the food bowl.

Our storeroom has an industrial sink, so I wheeled myself behind the sales counter and into the storeroom to fill his water. As I came back out, Matilda popped her head up from her adorable pink cuddle bed under the sales counter.

"Hey, baby girl!"

She pranced over to me and poked her nose at the water bowl, checking if it contained something tasty for her.

"You already had your breakfast, you silly girl. This is just water anyway." I gave her a few pats on the head and continued back toward Reginald. Matilda trotted along beside me, her gaze still fixed on the bowl.

Just as I opened the little kennel door, Matilda's front paws landed on my lap, sending the water bowl spinning across the tray—in slow motion, I swear. The bowl clanged against the lip of the tray and water sloshed all over my black lantern-sleeved sweater.

"Matilda!" I cried, but it was no use. Her attention was no longer on me or the water bowl.

No, she was staring at the now open kennel door, where a cream ball of fluff was deftly leaping through—this time in fast motion—onto a shelf of paw and nose cream for dogs.

Matilda's body went rigid for a quick second before she launched herself at the shelf.

"Matilda! Nooooooooooooooooo!"

Dawk came running over, dropping a clipboard he'd been holding. He tried to grab Matilda out of the air as she made a second attempt to reach Reginald, but he missed. The little dog's nose made contact with the cat's tail, sending Reginald fleeing across the tops of the shelves.

Like a little train of chaos, Matilda weaved between the shelves, Dawk on her tail, me forming the caboose with my wheelchair. Products rained down around us. Meows and barks filled the air.

We likely would have continued that way until the end of time if not for the voice that boomed through the store.

"WHAT IN THE BLOODY FANGS IS GOING ON IN HERE!?"

We all froze, cat and dog included.

There was only one human or vampire who could halt the never-ending feud between cats and dogs with just a simple call of her voice.

"Mom?"

All five feet of her strode forward, her boots on the concrete the only sound, but a sound formidable enough to keep us all in place.

With an unhurried movement, she reached up to where Reginald was caught mid-transition between a shelf of grain-free, egg-free, nut-free, dairy-free, fun-free dog treats and a display of sweaters that said "I Ruff You," and pulled him into her arms.

She stepped up to Matilda next. My dog rolled over and showed my mom her belly.

"Now," my mom said, looking between the two animals, "I don't know who started it, but this ends now."

She returned Reginald to his kennel and turned back to me and Dawk. "Well? Are you going to clean this up or just stare at me?"

Dawk, who had spent many a day at my house as a kid, regressed back to his six-year-old self with a quick, "Yes, ma'am."

I couldn't judge him, as I was grabbing as much collateral damage off the floor as I could too.

To her credit, my mom helped us put everything back in place. I'd lucked out. The only damage was a couple of crushed treat boxes, which I could give to Matilda. Dawk ran back to my office to record the waste while I rotated Zippy toward my mom.

"Thanks for grabbing Reginald before more of my store was destroyed."

"Of course, sweetie."

She moved behind me and pushed me back to the sales counter just as Dawk came back, looking a little sweaty.

"You look shaken up, my dear Dawk. But just wait until you hear this."

And then she stopped talking.

Seconds passed before Dawk took the bait. "Okay, Aunt Velma, what is it?"

"There's a killer on the loose."

Chapter Five

I'm sure my mom expected gasps and hands covering hearts, but Dawk and I knew her well enough to pick up on her exaggerative tone of voice.

I crossed my arms over my still-wet sweater. "Is there now?"

"Okay, okay, Jos. There isn't exactly a killer, but there is a maniac on the loose. I just heard from Roxie."

Hmm. Roxie was my grandmother's best friend, and she'd been known to call my mother up to gossip as well. She gossiped with anyone who would talk to her. You'd think that would make her words unreliable, but it was the opposite—she was somehow very accurate.

Dawk and I exchanged a look before we both said, "Tell us everything."

My mom gave us the whole telephone chain of how Roxie got the information, which could have been summed up as "one of the cops told their mom, and now everyone knows."

"The cops kept the first incident quiet, both to keep the rumor mill under control and to respect the privacy of the victim, but now there's been a second incident."

"What happened?" I asked.

My mom jumped up on the counter, getting comfortable to tell the tale. "Three nights ago, a student at Arteria Falls College was knocked out and physically assaulted in her apartment. Her roommate was out for the night, so no one was there to help. After they knocked her out, her assailant…," she paused for dramatic effect, "…*bit her* and *staked her* in the arm."

My mom finally got the gasps she'd wanted.

Vampires do not bite. We do not bite humans. We do not bite each other. Not only is it illegal, it's an unspoken code of honor between us. *No biting.* It's just too dangerous. We can't risk exposure of any kind, so we keep our fangs locked down unless we can't find the scissors and need to slice open a bag of chocolates.

And staking? Holy Dracula's cape. Staking was so far beyond reality that it's usually a comical topic for us.

"They staked her? In the arm? Wouldn't that have, I don't know, killed her entire arm?" I asked.

My mom shook her head. "No, they used a really thin stake. Roxie said it was about the size of those thick pencils they give little kids. But it was whittled to look all old and ominous."

"That's so weird," my cousin said. "Is the student okay?"

"Yes, other than what I'm sure is massive emotional damage, she's okay."

As soon as I knew the student was okay, my brain flipped into analytical mode. "Did she see anything? Was there any evidence left at the scene?"

"She didn't see anything, but get this," my mom said, her voice full of inappropriate delight, "they left a little paper heart at the scene. And the student recalled finding a heart on her front door a couple days before the attack."

I scrunched my brow. "A paper heart? Is that the attacker's calling card?"

"Apparently. They attacked again. Left another heart. Bit the victim. Staked them in the shoulder. But even more interesting…both victims have bright-blue eyes and light-blond hair."

Dawk and I looked at each other, taking in the other's hair and eyes.

"Fangs," we said.

Chapter Six

"Exactly," my mom said, triumphant in her storytelling. "Don't worry about it too much, though. There are lots of blond-haired and blue-eyed vamps in town."

"Yeah, but you said *bright* blue and *light* blond," Dawk noted, his pale skin somehow getting even paler. "My girlfriend is blond and blue-eyed too, but darker shades. I hope that means she's safe, but with only two victims, we can't be sure of the pattern yet."

Dawk had a new girlfriend of two months, Everly. She was from Arteria Falls originally, but had moved to Fangstaff, Arizona, with her parents many years ago. The whole family had recently returned to be closer to Everly's grandparents.

I wheeled up to squeeze his arm. "You sound like me, talking about criminal patterns. All my PI babbling must have rubbed off on you."

He gave me a weak smile, but worry was written all over his face.

My mom patted the counter. "Come sit down, kid. It will be okay. I mean, it's not like any of you have received a heart."

It was my turn to pale. I rushed to the front of the shop and hit the button to open the door. I plucked the red heart I'd noticed the day before off the glass.

My mom's face fell when she saw it. "Someone left that on the door?"

I nodded. "I thought someone was just being cute by leaving a little heart on the door…but now I'm not so sure." I handed it to my mom.

Her whole demeanor changed. This was no longer gossip. My mom might have been a lot of things—loud, rude, unfiltered—but she was also fiercely protective.

She jumped off the counter, leaving the heart behind. "We can't know for sure, but we need to assume this is from the attacker. You two need to be careful."

Dawk hurried into the storeroom to call his girlfriend while I rolled behind the counter to grab a notepad. "Tell me everything you know about the second victim."

Roxie's Rumor Mill hadn't turned up much info on the second victim yet. All my mom knew was that the victim was a man this time. His wife was out of town, so he'd been all alone in the house. He didn't see the attacker either. The only differences between the two attacks seemed to be the gender of the victim and the stake location. One in the arm, one in the shoulder.

I wrote everything down. I wasn't about to start investigating just because we *might* have received a heart from the attacker. There were hearts all over Arteria Falls. Isa's Eats was covered in Valentine's banners, and little heart centerpieces sat on each table. The Bloody Grape, the blood-and-wine bar, had little heart-shaped sticky notepads on every table so (hopefully) single patrons could give out their phone numbers. Even Out for Blood, my favorite blood bodega, had their front window painted with a Valentine's scene.

But I wanted to be prepared in case the situation escalated.

A customer came in looking for a nail trimmer, so my mom said goodbye with a promise to find out everything else she could about the attacks.

The store stayed fairly busy for the rest of the afternoon, so Dawk and I didn't have much time to discuss the situation, just long enough for him to tell me Everly hadn't received a heart.

Around four o'clock, when we hit a lull, Dawk gathered his things. "I'm off to soccer practice. I stocked everything up, so you should be fine for the rest of the afternoon."

"Thanks, favorite cousin. I hope you have fun with your sports-balls activities." Dawk was a soccer fiend and played all year. During the cold Colorado winter, he played indoors.

"Me too. I'm hoping it takes my mind off the attacks."

I nodded. "I know you're worried, but we should both try not to freak out. Just lock your door extra tight tonight."

"Right, because there's an *extra tight* setting on my lock."

With that, he gave me a small wave and left.

I took a deep breath and wheeled around the store. Friday afternoons were slow. People had better things to do than shop for their pets, so I was fine working the two hours until six o'clock alone.

Well, except for Matilda and Reginald of course.

"Reginald, what do you think about these atta—"

My question was cut off by the ding-dong of the front door.

"Welcome to Matilda's VamPets," I called out as I angled my chair toward the door. "Oh, it's just you, Dawk. Did you forget something?"

Silently, he held up a red heart.

I sighed. "I take it that's not the one we already had?"

"Nope. It was on my windshield. Is it time to freak out now?"

"Fang it." I rolled up and plucked it out of his hand. "Come on."

I led him back to the sales counter, where I'd stored the original heart in a drawer.

Side by side, they looked exactly the same.

Same shade of red, same glue on the back, and both were made of construction paper…because, apparently, the attacker was five years old.

"We need to tell the police."

I used the shop telephone—a light-pink cordless model—to call the non-emergency line. I had to hold for quite a bit before a gruff detective quickly took the information. Hearts were popping up all over town, he said, so they couldn't act on every instance. They were doing their best, but the calls were overwhelming them.

Great.

I explained the situation to Dawk. "Lots of hearts are being left. That makes the probability of you being the next target pretty low. I think you should just go to soccer practice and not worry about this."

He started to protest, but I cut him off, "Let me worry about this, okay? You know I've got your back, right?"

His fingers found their way through his hair, his default stress maneuver, but he said, "I know. You always have."

"That's right. Remember when I beat up that kid who kept stealing your blood bags when you were in third grade?"

He cracked a smile for the first time in hours. "I'll never forget the sound his nose made when your fist connected with it."

"My thumb dislocated. I didn't know you were supposed to keep it on the outside of your fist when you throw a punch."

"That's right! Your mom shoved it back in and then yelled at us both for, like, twenty minutes."

"It was worth it. I'll punch this attacker for you too, if needed."

Dawk squeezed my shoulder. "Maybe let me do the punching this time."

"If you insist," I said with a shrug.

With that, he went to practice.

I helped the occasional customer and made sure Reginald was stocked up on food and water, but I spent most of the afternoon thinking.

What could I do? I barely knew anything.

The attacker was probably quick and nimble when they left the two hearts.

Even if I could find nearby businesses with security cameras, the likelihood that I could see the street well enough to spot the attacker was very small. People crawled all over Vein Street all day. The attacker would be just another passing blur.

I tapped my pen on the counter. There was only one thing to do. I had to talk to the victims.

My mom hadn't known their names, so I pulled out my phone to text a contact I'd been developing at the police station. With my investigation into Grandpa Roan back on, I'd figured it couldn't hurt to have a buddy at the station.

Luckily, several officers frequented my boutique, so over the last few months, I'd gotten friendly with them and assessed who'd be a good contact for me.

The winner was Dean Quall, a thirty-something vampire who was fairly new to the force. In the past, he'd come into the shop alone to grab supplies for his dog. When he came in just before Halloween, I'd convinced him to buy his little Maltese a costume. He'd chosen an adorable pink princess costume. Before he left, I'd made him swear to bring me pictures.

When he did, I'd encouraged him to bring his dog to the shop, promising her a bag of free treats. I'd fawned all over the little white pup. It had been blessedly slow in the shop, so I asked him about his life, his work, sharing my own stories too.

On his next visit, I'd invited him to volunteer at an event the shelter was hosting. We'd had plenty of time to talk while manning a donation station, allowing our friendship to grow.

You might be thinking, *friendship—weren't you using him, Josie?* You'd be right. I enjoyed his company, but ultimately I was developing a contact. I felt bad, but a vamp's gotta do what a vamp's gotta do, am I right?

I pulled out my phone to text Dean, telling him I was concerned about the situation given my own blond hair and blue eyes.

Dean was concerned too, so getting information from him was easy. Most of it I already knew, like that I should double-check all my locks before bedtime because the attacks happened at night, but I also managed to wheedle the name of the first victim out of him—Maggie Dodson.

Chapter Seven

"Brrrr. It's still so cold in the van, Matilda. I swear the heater isn't doing anything. At least we aren't out in the wind, though."

Matilda and I turned onto my street fifteen minutes after six o'clock hit. The last half hour had been slow, so everything had been clean and ready to go when I'd locked the door at six.

I was exhausted by the time I pulled into the driveway. My back was killing me. I'd spent most of the day on the sales floor, rather than in my office, which meant I'd been in my wheelchair almost all day.

Zippy was great and I was so grateful to have her in my life, but sitting in the same chair all day was painful, not to mention the toll wheeling around took on my upper body. My shoulders were so sore and my wrists were throbbing.

"Matilda," I told her as I unloaded my chair, "I think I should take a nice, long bath. What do you think?"

She just wagged her whole body at me from her seat in the van, excited to be home.

"I'll take that as a 'yes.' I've got an hour until Elm is supposed to come over to watch *Nosferatu*. Don't worry, I'll put a bowl of your favorite Blue Buffalo food down first."

I let her jump out of the car, and she ran up to the porch to check her plants.

Chuckling at my ridiculous dog as she inserted her nose into a blue spruce, I followed her to the porch…where something red caught my eye.

Right in the middle of the door, just below the peephole, was a red heart.

Fangs.

I plucked it and instantly noticed that it felt a bit different than the other two hearts I'd held. The paper was smoother—not construction paper.

After dropping my keys in a rush to unlock the door, I let us inside and rolled straight to the dining table. Not even bothering to take off my bomber jacket, I pulled the other two hearts out of the front pocket of my backpack.

All three in a row, I examined them. They were about the same size and very similar shades of red, but along with the paper type, the glue also looked different on the new heart.

I rubbed my fingers across the back of each heart, letting the tips graze the glue. The new heart indeed used different glue—something thinner yet stickier.

What in the bloody bite? Did the attacker run out of construction paper *and* glue? It was possible. Maybe they'd switched to the stickier glue to ensure the hearts didn't get lost in the wind.

A snowstorm was expected to hit in a few days. The temperatures had been dropping, and the wind rising. It was perfectly reasonable that the attacker would want to make the hearts stickier. They also could have run out of paper or switched for some other reason…but it just felt odd to me.

Criminal calling cards were usually very consistent. That was the point of a calling card, after all.

There was no point speculating, though, so I moved on. My phone had fallen to the bottom of my backpack, but once I managed to find it below eighty receipts and two dozen empty bags from Isa's (I loved the chocolate-coconut balls, okay?), I pulled up the doorbell app. I might not have had a camera at the shop to catch who left the heart on the door, but I did have a doorbell camera at home.

I tapped on the motion log for the day. Lots of cars passing. The mailwoman. Several dogs being walked. A runner or two. But no one approached the house.

Frickin' fangs. What was the point of the camera if I couldn't see who was leaving things on my door? How had the note-leaver from a few months back and the heart-leaver from today gotten around the camera? And what were the chances that would happen to me with two different sources?

Could they be related? Was the attacker the same person taunting me about my grandfather?

No, that didn't feel right. The two instances weren't related, they'd just both found a way around the camera.

Maybe I should add seventy more cameras to cover every possible angle.

After forty minutes spent researching the cost of more cameras, the front door opened. Elm, Lynnae, and Calder walked in, bringing a gust of frigid wind with them.

"Ahhhh!" I cried as the hearts went flying around the room.

Elm ran forward to snag one just before it fell into Matilda's water bowl, Matilda chasing after them with a *I don't know why we're running but I love it* look on her face. Lynnae picked one up off the navy-and-white rug underneath the table. The last one stuck itself to a snake plant. Calder snatched it off and offered it to me with a little bow. "Your heart, m'lady."

His cold hand grazed mine as I took it.

Calder giving me a heart.

The significance of that was not lost on me. I gulped as I nodded at him. "Thanks, Cal."

He just smiled and set a growler on the table. "We come bearing gifts. Bloody gifts."

Elm turned the growler to read the sticker that'd been haphazardly slapped on. "Oh my stars! This is my favorite blend from The Bloody Grape. Dark chocolate and espresso in an A+ blood Cabernet. You know the way to my heart, Calder." They leaned back, clutching their chest.

"Excuse you," Lynnae said, grabbing a seat next to me at the table. "I picked it out. Calder wanted to try the new mint blend, but I knew this was a chocolate kind of night."

"Wait, the three of you didn't go together?"

Elm went to the kitchen to grab four wine glasses. "Naw, I just got here the same time they did." The kitchen was open to the living room and the small dining area, so we could still see them as they held the glasses up. "Do these work?"

Three were plain, but the fourth said "WINE: Because biting people is illegal."

I held my hands out. "I'll take the biting people glass. It's highly appropriate for the day I've had."

"Oh?" Calder asked, a cheeky grin on his face. "Did you feel like biting someone?"

I raised an eyebrow. "You wish."

Lynnae cleared her throat in a long and exaggerated manner that went something like this: Ehhheeemmmemmmm*cough*eeemmm*cough*emmm.

"Sorry, she said. There must have been a bat in my throat."

I shook my head at her and picked up the three hearts. "It's not who I want to bite, it's who wants to bite me. And Dawk."

Chapter Eight

"Wait." Elm came to sit on my other side, the glasses clinking on the table. They stared at the hearts. "You aren't doing crafts, are you, Jos? I heard about the attacks."

Calder stiffened, and Lynnae reached for the growler. "Okay, it sounds like we need to distribute this now."

As Lynnae poured the glasses, Calder picked up the hearts. "What attacks? Who wants to bite you, Jos? And what in the fangs do these hearts have to do with it?" His voice was tense and scratchy.

"How have you two not heard about this yet?"

My roommate shrugged. "We were doing an autopsy today. They're time-consuming and intense."

Calder and Lynnae are anatomy researchers at Arteria Falls College. Our town is too small to have it's own medical examiner, so Calder and Lynnae fill that roll in addition to their research.

"Makes sense." After a long sigh, I settled in to tell them what I knew.

I wrapped up the story by explaining, "With the doorbell camera failing me, I definitely need to talk to Maggie Dodson. Talking to her will be a good first step. I didn't want to push Dean to give me the second victim's name…it just felt like too much to ask at once. I'll have to finesse it out of him another time."

Elm picked their glass up. "I can help you with that. You were so methodical, I didn't want to interrupt your story and throw you off. But I know the second victim."

I grabbed onto their arm, almost causing their glass to topple. "What? Tell me everything! And why is your sweater so soft?"

With a laugh, Elm explained, "My aunt knit it for me! I don't know where she found this yarn, but the deep purple really brings out my eyes. You can borrow it, but let's talk about that later. Calder looks like he's about to snap over there."

Calder, indeed, did look like he was about to crush his glass. Now sitting in the seat across from me, he kept shooting me and the hearts heated looks.

"The victim works with me at First Blood in the accounting department," Elm said.

First Blood is the vampire world's biggest blood supplier. Elm worked there researching blood bag delivery methods.

"We eat lunch together sometimes and play foosball in the break room," Elm continued. "His boss isn't known for discretion, so the whole company knew what happened by nine this morning."

"Hang on a sec." I dug a notebook and a pen out of my backpack. With a hand flourish, I said. "Proceed."

Elm knew the whole story, as the victim's gossipy boss had gone to see them at the hospital before work and had extracted all the details.

The victim, Niall Haddock, had fallen asleep on the couch. With his wife out of town, he'd stayed up late watching TV. He'd woken up eventually and decided to move to his bed. On the way there, his cat hissed from behind him, but before he could fully turn around, something collided with his head. When he woke up on the floor, his cat was curled up on his chest, a stake was wedged in his shoulder, and blood was leaking from his neck…onto a red paper heart. He had no idea who had attacked him or why.

"I take it there was no security system?"

Elm shrugged. "I don't know."

"Do you know when he'll be released from the hospital?"

"No, but some of us were talking about going to see him tomorrow if he's still there."

My eyes lit up and before I could ask, Elm put a hand on my shoulder. "Yes, you can come with us. Just don't make me look bad in front of my coworkers."

I snorted. "You mean I shouldn't use a pack of wet wipes as an excuse to tag along with you?"

"Please, for the Goddess' sake, do not."

Back in October, when I'd been investigating my favorite customer's murder, I'd needed to see someone at Elm's Dungeons & Dragons game and had used returning a pack of wet wipes to Elm as an excuse to interrupt their game. Elm hadn't been thrilled about it, for reasons unbeknownst to me.

Lynnae drained her glass and set it down a little too hard on the table.

"Enough of this dreariness. We can talk about who's trying to attack all the blonds later. Let's go watch the movie." She stood up and grabbed the growler. "Elm, come sit by me. I need to feel this sweater."

As Elm and Lynnae sat down, Lynnae in our puffy purple armchair and Elm in our navy-blue wingback chair, I couldn't help but notice they left the couch for me and Calder. A mischievous glint in Lynnae's eye confirmed my theory.

I dumped everything on the table into my backpack. "Let me just put this away and grab my crutch." My adrenaline had made me forget the pain while at the table, but now I *really* needed to get out of the wheelchair. My hips and butt were killing me.

Calder grabbed my backpack. "Can I help?" he asked tentatively.

He knew I didn't need help. Realizing he wanted to talk to me about something, I nodded.

I rolled Zippy to my room, Matilda trotting along behind me. She jumped on my bed and curled up on my pillow.

"Where should I put this?" Calder asked from the doorway.

"On my desk chair is fine."

I unzipped my bomber jacket, which I'd forgotten to take off, and tossed it next to Matilda.

"What's up, Cal?"

He shifted, one of his sneakers squeaking on the wood floor. "Are you doing anything on Tuesday?"

I thought through my schedule. "I don't think so…wait. Tuesday?"

Calder's cheeks reddened just a tad. It was so adorable that I could have died right there.

Tuesday was Valentine's Day.

"Just working," I continued. "We've got a zillion people picking up cakes."

He nodded. "So you're free after work?"

Horror, nerves, and excitement blended on high speed in my stomach. Was this it? Was he finally asking me out?

We'd gone to a concert in Denver a couple months back. Calder had been so thoughtful about helping me with Zippy. He had even stayed seated the whole concert, despite everyone around us standing and screaming. There's no way I could have stood for more than a couple minutes, so he'd spent the concert sitting next to me.

I'd been nervous beforehand, wondering if he would make a move that night, but he hadn't. We'd just enjoyed each other's company.

Afterward, we'd had to stay the night in Denver, but he had just dropped me off at my hotel room, squeezed my shoulder, and gone to his room.

So was this the moment? I knew it was coming soon. The line of tension between us had grown so much over the years that it was about to snap.

But was I ready? My Grandma Margie had said something to me a few months back. *"You know, Josie, those who love us, love us. All of us. Our passions, our obsessions, our perfections, our flaws. They love the spark inside of us. Keeping yourself from them…isn't just hard on you. It's hard on them too. I know you think you're a burden, but you're not. Let yourself be loved."*

Those words had danced through my brain every time I saw Calder. I knew she was right. But was I ready? My grandmother said I wasn't a burden, but I still felt like one.

Calder drew me back to the moment as he said, even more uncertain then, "Josie? Are you free after work?"

"Oh, sorry, Cal! Yes, I'm free."

He smiled, his dimple making an appearance. "Great. I was wondering if you want to come over to make that blood blend we were talking about? Pickles, coconut water, and B+ in a Malbec? I've got a ton of coconut water."

Relief and a hint of disappointment flowed through me that he hadn't asked for an official date. Not wanting him to see either emotion, I put a big grin on my face. "That sounds amazing. Let's do it."

It was his turn to feel relieved. His body instantly relaxed. "Awesome. Maybe we can watch a movie too."

"Of course, but I'm bringing Matilda to snuggle with."

"I wouldn't have it any other way."

"Don't be surprised if I fall asleep during the movie, though. I'm going to be dead on my wheels after helping Isa all night on Monday. Oh! That reminds me."

I stood up and grabbed my forearm crutch. After clenching my butt a few times to help with the pain, I walked to the living room.

"Sooooooooooo," I said, my eyes moving between my three friends. "I maybe, kinda-sorta, definitely volunteered all of you to help us make all the dog cakes on Monday night. Sorry, not sorry!"

Calder laughed, Elm groaned, and Lynnae gave me a death stare.

"It will be fun! And just think, we can eat all the leftover vampire treats at the bakery." Elm and Lynnae raised their eyebrows at me, unimpressed. "And I'll buy you all several rounds of drinks at The Bloody Grape."

That did the trick.

Chapter Nine

*K*nock knock knock. "Ow!"

In my excitement to be at Maggie Dodson's first-floor apartment, I knocked way too hard, causing my wrist to subluxate, which is a partial dislocation—just one of the many lovely symptoms of my Hypermobile Ehlers-Danlos Syndrome. The hypermobile aspect means that my connective tissue is loose and stretchy due to faulty collagen, causing chronic pain and my joints to move out of place, among other things.

Luckily, everything slipped right back where it belonged just as the door opened.

Rubbing my wrist, I asked, "Maggie Dodson?"

She bit her lip, looking nervous, before she spit out, "Whoareyou?" The words came out in one jumble.

The young woman before me looked frazzled. Her dull-brown turtleneck sweater was worn at the cuffs where she was twisting her fingers around the fabric.

Long, tangled, light-blond hair spilled out from a simple black beanie. Black circles rimmed tense bright-blue eyes.

This must be Maggie and not the roommate.

Holding up my left hand, I reached toward my back pocket with my right. "Don't be alarmed. I'm going to pull my identification out of my pocket. I'm a private investigator."

She didn't object, so I pulled out my PI badge. "As you can see, I'm legit. My name is Josie. Are you Maggie?"

She nodded.

"Can I come in?"

She shook her head.

Fangs. I hadn't thought about what I'd do if she wouldn't let me in. I'd left Zippy in the car, needing a break from the chair. The walk to her door wasn't long, and there weren't any stairs, so I'd figured I'd be okay to use my crutch…but I could only stand for so long. The wind was starting to pick up as well.

I looked around, my van catching my eye. "Could we go talk at my van? I just need to sit down. You can stay outside the van, though."

She looked at it, assessing the danger. "There's no one else in there?"

"Nope." Matilda was at the shop with Dawk and Lacey. It was Saturday and would likely be busy, but Dawk pushed me out the door to investigate. Literally, he pushed me outside and loaded my wheelchair for me.

Maggie still looked suspicious, but she eyed my crutch for a few seconds and nodded.

I led the way and opened the side door on the passenger side—Matilda's side. It was a good thing I wore black pants that day, as Matilda's fur coated the seat.

As soon as my butt hit the fabric, Maggie was on me. "How did you find me? What do you want?"

I couldn't exactly tell her that Roxie's Rumor Mill had come through for me. I'd texted my mom the night before and asked if she could help me find Maggie. By this morning, I'd learned that so-and-so's cousin, who worked with so-and-so, knew so-and-so, who had a daughter who lived in Maggie's complex. One of those so-and-sos sent the address and apartment number through the chain.

"As a PI, I have resources to help me locate people. I'm here to discuss the incident from a few nights ago."

Maggie reached for her left arm, grabbing her bicep. She winced.

"Is that the injury?"

She nodded. My eyes moved to her neck, but her turtleneck obscured any sign of a bite.

"Are you just here to gawk at me?" she asked with narrowed eyes.

"No, of course not. I'm investigating the attacker and have some questions for you. I would greatly appreciate any information you can provide."

Her eyes slid over my hair before connecting with my own eyes. "You got a heart, didn't you?"

I bit my lip. I normally wouldn't reveal such information, but I got the feeling it might help build camaraderie with her. With a sigh, I answered, "Yes. My cousin got one too. We each got two, actually." I didn't know if that first heart was for me or Dawk or both, so I was going with both.

"Okay, I'll talk to you. I don't want this happening to anyone else. The more people looking for this bloodsucker, the better."

Bloodsucker was an apt name, considering the attacker was biting their victims.

"Thank you so much, Maggie." I pulled out my small notepad—one of those you can write on in the rain. The pages started to flap in the wind, so I leaned further back in the van. "Can you walk me through the attack?"

I don't think she expected such a broad question. Her hands immediately flew to her beanie, tugging it down to almost cover her eyes, as if she could protect herself by concealing as much of her as possible. "Umm…"

"Take a breath, Maggie. Let's do it together."

We both breathed in and out. "Good. Just go slow. Start at the beginning. I understand your roommate was gone?"

"Yeah. I was alone that night. I don't really remember that much. Something woke me up...I assume a noise. I didn't think anything of it, so I got up to use the bathroom. When I came out, I felt something hit my head. Everything went black."

"And when you woke up?" I prompted.

She took a shaky breath, and her eyes glistened. "I was on the floor in the living room. My arm was in agony, so I didn't even notice my neck at first. I started screaming. My neighbor heard me, so they called the cops and ran over. The door was unlocked, so he came right in. He told me not to move and asked if my head was bleeding. I was confused. With my right arm, I felt the back of my head. It was sore, but I didn't feel any blood. But then I ran my hand to the ends of my hair and felt the blood. The sting in my neck wasn't that painful, but when I felt the two holes...I freaked out. Then the cops showed up."

I reached out to squeeze her arm but thought better of it. "That must have been so hard, so scary."

A single tear escaped her eye. "It was. So scary. Especially once I came home from the hospital. What if they come back to finish me off? Do you think they will?" she asked, the desperation clear in her voice.

"I honestly don't know, Maggie. As they've now attacked someone new, I would think they've moved on from you, but we can't be sure. You need to be careful."

She snorted. "The second attack doesn't exactly make me feel better. But, yeah, I'm being careful. So careful that I'm not sleeping at all." That explained the black circles under her eyes. "I bought pepper spray and a taser."

"Good. Just make sure you know how to use them. Is there anywhere else you can stay for now?"

Maggie started twisting her sweater cuffs again. "No. I'm all alone here. Arteria Falls is new for me. I came for school. And my family…well, let's just say they weren't about to jump on a plane to come to see me."

I winced. Even after a violent attack, her family didn't come see her? "That's so rough. I'm sorry you're feeling alone. What about your roommate?"

"She stays at her girlfriend's house a lot, but now she's so freaked out that she's staying there every night. We get along okay, but we aren't exactly friends anyway. Found each other on a notice board."

An idea struck me. "Maybe you can apply for temporary student housing. If there's a dorm room available, at least you would be somewhere different."

Her eyes lit up, a smidge of hope budding. "I hadn't thought of that." She looked ready to run back to her apartment to fill out an application.

"I have just a few more questions if that's okay?"

Maggie waved her hand, signaling me to continue.

I checked my list of questions. "What did the assailant hit you with?"

"I have no idea. It wasn't something of mine, as far as the police can tell."

So the attacker brought their own weapon. Interesting.

"How did they get in your apartment?"

She gestured to her door. "Picked the lock."

This attacker was prepared.

"Can you think of anyone who would want to hurt you?"

Maggie shook her head. "No. The police asked that too, obviously, but there's no one. I mostly keep to myself."

"No one who has an issue with you?"

Her expression turned thoughtful. "Well, I'm one of the top students in anthropology. I just love studying vampire culture and ancient vampire sites. Anyway, there's another student, Colleen, who hates me. She's really competitive and resents me."

"For your grades?"

She started ticking things off on her fingers. "Yes, for my grades, the internship I won for this summer, how much I get along with all the staff and professors."

"Gotcha. She's jealous. Do you think she would do something like this?"

Maggie sighed. "No. I don't think she's this devious. At least, I hope not. And if it is her, why the second attack?"

Shrugging, I said, "I don't know, but I have to take the whole picture into account. So, you've told me about school. Do you have any other activities or friends I should know about?"

"I'm boring. It's just school and yoga for me."

"Yoga at Vampyasa?"

Maggie smiled for the first time. "Yes! I love it so much. It really helps me unwind. I should probably go soon…maybe it will help my nerves. I'd have to avoid using my injured arm, though."

"That's a great idea! What time do you go?"

A huge wind blew through. I grabbed my hair to keep it from tangling, while Maggie grabbed the already-tangled strands sticking out from under her hat.

"Noon on Tuesday and Thursday!" she shouted over the wind.

"Thanks," I called back. "Has anyone ever threatened you? Not just recently, but ever?"

"No!"

"I understand the assailant left something behind?"

She stepped closer to hear me better. "Yeah, a heart and a little metal object. It looks like an old-style scale. You know, with two sides that had to balance."

A scale? That certainly hadn't made it into Roxie's rumor mill yet. "Do you have any idea why the scale?"

"None. The police asked me too, but I have absolutely no clue."

Was it somehow important to the attacker then? Could it represent the scales of justice? Perhaps they thought they were bringing about justice. "Okay, I can think about that more later. Did you get any hearts before the attack?"

"One on the front door—we thought it was from my roommate's girlfriend. One on our little mailbox too."

"Last thing. I assume the police took the hearts you received, so can you look at these for me?"

I inched my butt even farther back on the seat, trying to get as far away from the wind's clutches as possible. Taking the hearts out of my backpack, I said, "Can you tell me if these look familiar?"

Maggie leaned in. "These two," she said, pointing to the construction paper hearts.

"You're sure?"

"Yes. Even the one from that night looked like those." She rubbed her arms, getting cold in the wind.

"Thanks so much, Maggie. That's it for now, but can I have your number in case I have more questions?" She looked hesitant, so I added, "I can't tell you how much I appreciate your help."

After reciting her number, she took a deep breath. "Just find them, okay? And be safe."

With that, she ran back to her apartment.

Chapter Ten

Hospital floors and wheelchair tires aren't the best combination when you're a bored vampire spinning 'round and 'round in your chair. The nurse at the desk looked about two seconds away from popping her fangs out if I made one more *squeak*.

I smiled and stopped moving…my chair at least. My hands started playing a beat on my legs instead.

"Excuse me," the nurse said, clearly not amused with the sick beat I was playing. "Are you here to see someone?"

"Yes, ma'am—Niall Haddock. He has some other visitors right now, though, so I figured I'd wait."

She eyed me over her glasses. "I see. Let's hope, for both our sakes, that they aren't in there for *too long*."

Well, not everyone can be a Josie fan.

Lucky for her, Elm and his colleagues exited the room just a few minutes later. As they passed, Elm gave me a small salute and a wink.

I chuckled and waved. Bad Josie, the little vampire who sits on my right shoulder, won out against Good Josie as I let my wheels loose and peeled out with a huge *squeak*…or maybe it was a *squawk*.

"Whoops!" I said with all the pleasantness possible.

I swear the nurse snarled at me as I wheeled by.

Niall's eyes slowly opened when I knocked on the door. Confusion clouded his sky-blue eyes when he saw me.

"Erm, can I help you?"

The pleasantness in my voice was genuine this time. "Hello, Niall! My name is Josie. I'm a private investigator."

"Oh. Well, I don't think I need a PI. The police are on it, so…" he trailed off as I shook my head.

"I'm not here to sell my services." I waved a hand over my hair. "My cousin and I both got hearts."

Niall flinched. "Fangs. That's sucks." He gestured to his neck where a bandage undoubtedly covered the bite marks. "I would know."

With a smile, I rolled a bit closer. "Did you just make a morbid joke? I love it."

He nodded. "Yeah, my wife's always saying to look on the bite side, so I figure I should try not to be too miserable right now."

"The *bite* side?"

"Her vampire jokes aren't that great." His toothy grin made it clear that he thought his wife was absolutely adorable.

I chuckled. "I thought it was *bloody good*. Can I come in?"

"I give you permission to cross the threshold."

"Ooo, you better be careful which vampires you let in…"A flush spread across my cheeks. "Oh my stars, I'm sorry, that was insensitive, given the situation."

Niall waved me off. "Don't worry about it. How can I help?"

I pulled my notebook from my backpack, which hung on the back of Zippy. "As I'm sure you've deduced, I'm trying to identify the culprit before they strike again. Do you mind taking me through the attack?"

He blew out a breath. "Yeah, that's fine. My wife is out of town—she's been trying to get a flight back ever since, but there's snow in Boise—and so I was alone in the house. Just me and our cat, Sammy. I passed out on the couch watching *Love is Blind*. Goddess, human drama is addicting."

I snorted. "Don't I know it. *Married at First Sight* keeps me up all night."

"Right? Anyway, I got up to get a glass of water and move to the bedroom. Just as I reached the kitchen, Sammy hissed behind me. I started to turn and—"

SMACK. He slammed a fist into the opposite palm. "Wanna see?"

I grimaced. I didn't really want to look at the back of his head, but he was leaning forward and rubbing his short blond hair, so I went for it.

Upon rolling closer, I told him, "Wow. That's quite the bump. Did it bleed?"

"Nope, but when I woke up there was blood everywhere from my shoulder and my neck."

I held my breath, scared he was about to rip his bandages off to show me the wounds.

But he moved on. "Sammy had his claws dug into my shirt, clearly trying to protect me while I was knocked out. I noticed the stake first." He gave me a very serious look. "I do not recommend a stake to the shoulder."

"How big was the stake?" I hadn't thought to ask Maggie.

"It was thin…not your *Buffy the Vampire Slayer* stake. Maybe as thick as my ring finger?"

I wrote down, *As thick as an average-sized dude's ring finger*. "Tell me more. Did you call the cops?"

"Yep. My phone was in my pocket. The officers who showed up were a bit freaked out, talking about this being the second attack." His expression grew serious again, but *seriously* serious this time. "They told me some poor student was attacked. How traumatizing at such a young age."

Hmm. I bet he would be a bit traumatized too once he processed things more, but I didn't say that. "I talked to her earlier. She's not doing too well. I think once we get the attacker in custody, she'll feel a lot better."

He bobbed his head in acknowledgment. "You better ask me more questions then."

"What did the attacker hit you with?"

"Not a clue."

"Okay, did the assailant leave anything behind?"

Niall pinched his brows together. "Yeah. He left a heart and…"

"And?" I leaned forward, my heart beating. Was it another mysterious symbol of justice?

"A little ceramic shield. It looks like it broke off a ceramic figure or something."

What the fangs? "Does that have any significance to you?"

He sighed. "Nope. I asked my wife too. She doesn't get it either."

Maybe it was something else important to the attacker. A shield and a scale. Shielding justice? That didn't make sense. I'd have to think on it later. "Back to the heart they left behind, had you received any hearts prior to the incident?"

"One on the front door—I thought my wife left it on her way out for her trip—and one on my back windshield."

Windshields, doors, a mailbox. All easily accessible places that the victims didn't think twice about. If the attacker had left one on Niall's pillow, perhaps with an Andes mint, that probably would have set off alarm bells.

I pulled the hearts out of my backpack. "Can you tell me if they looked like any of these?"

He curled his lip. "Those two. Those are the little jerks."

Of course, it was the construction paper hearts. Maybe the attacker ran out of paper after all. Who knew?

I did know that I needed something better to call them in my head than 'attacker' or its various synonyms.

They-of-the-Paper-Hearts? Too long.

Paper-Taper? Naw, they were using glue, not tape.

Paper-Heartie? Too cutesy.

I guess "attacker" it was.

After putting the hearts away, I consulted my question list.

"How did they get inside?"

"They picked the lock on the back door." That aligned with Maggie's answer.

"Can you think of anyone who would want to hurt you?"

He shook his head, the fluorescent lighting reflecting off his bright-blond hair.

"No one in town who has a problem with you? You haven't had any issues with anyone, or been threatened by anyone? No arguments? It doesn't have to be recent."

He leaned his head back on the hospital bed, thinking. "Not really. I know a lot of people in town—I've lived here my whole life—but I generally get along with people. Except my mother-in-law, but she's a little old human…so, no fangs." He sat up. "There was this one guy who really irked me. Maybe a month ago, we got into a huge fight."

My adrenaline spiked. "Tell me everything."

"I'm generally pretty patient. As I said, I live on the bite side of life. We only get 150 years on earth, why waste it being grumpy and angry? But we all lose control sometimes."

"Of course," I said, hoping he would hurry the story along.

"I was already having a bad day before encountering this guy. My cat threw up everywhere, I couldn't find my phone charger, and my boss gave me a ton of extra work. Then, after work, this vampire almost hit me with his car while I was on my bike." Niall gazed at the ceiling, his anger building. "Then the same guy kept knocking into me and actually toppled my water bottle, which leaked everywhere. But what really set me off was his creepy as fangs staring at some of the women."

"Wait, I'm confused." I held a hand up. "Was this all in a parking lot or something?"

"Oh, sorry," Niall said, looking back down at me. "It was at Vampyasa."

Chapter Eleven

"Vampyasa?" That was the second time I'd heard that name today. In my excitement, my spine straightened a little too fast. "Frick!"

Niall looked concerned. "Are you okay?"

"Yeah, sorry. My back just got a little upset for a second, but I'm okay. So, Vampyasa. Do you go there often?"

He smiled. "Yep, its my 'me' time. I love it there. Willow is such a good teacher."

"I've never been, but I've heard good things from my friend Elm. They rave about the classes." I'd also heard many good things from the ninety people who suggested I go to yoga to fix my body. You might be thinking, *That seems like a nice suggestion, Josie.* It does seem nice, but as I'm hypermobile, yoga stretches out my connective tissue too much, which causes me more pain, so it's a hard pass for me. It's also a bit frustrating when people make suggestions to *fix* my body. The word itself is offensive, as is the idea that I hadn't thought of a magical solution like yoga.

"They have a restorative class you might like." I tensed, afraid he was about to tell me yoga would "fix me." "You basically just prop yourself up with a million pillows and go into a meditative state."

I relaxed. Pillows and mediation? That actually sounded quite nice. "I'll talk to my physical therapist about it. Back to the story, what time do you go to yoga?"

"After work at 5:00 p.m. on Monday, Wednesday, and Friday."

Hmm, not the same time or days as Maggie. "Tell me about the fight. Was it physical?"

"Not really, mostly verbal. The dude—I don't know his name, so I'm going with 'dude'—positioned his mat next to mine. I don't think he noticed I was the cyclist he almost hit. After a few minutes, I realized he chose that spot for his mat so he could stare at the woman in front of us."

Niall scowled. "He knocked into me and my water bottle because he was staring at her instead of watching his space. I've seen plenty of other dudes looking at the women in class, but like, keep it subtle, you know? At the end of class, he rolled up his mat while staring down her shirt. He licked his lips, unconsciously, I think. She caught him and looked grossed out. I made a noise of disgust and shook my head at him. He didn't like that."

Niall sat up straight, really into the story. "Yoga mat under his arm, he marched up to me. Our argument went something like this:

"The dude says, 'Do you have a problem?'

"I say, 'Yeah, I do. You need to keep your eyes to yourself. And watch your space better on the mat.'

"Then the dude gets in my face and goes, 'Maybe keep your opinions to yourself.'"

Niall held a hand in front of his face.

"So then I basically push my nose into his and say, 'You asked, buddy.'"

Niall shoved his hand into his nose.

"Then the dude grabs my shirt."

Niall grabbed his own hospital gown.

"I'm like, 'You do not want to go there. Trust me.'

"Then the dude lets go of my shirt, pushes me back, and says, 'You better shut your mouth, or I'll shut it for you.'"

Niall dropped the gown and whipped backward.

"And that's when some dude and Willow pushed between us. She told us to stop or she'd kick us out permanently."

He gave me a little bow that signaled the end of his story. Unable to resist his charm, I clapped my hands.

"Bravo, sir. Have you seen this dude in class again? And do you remember seeing him there before that day?"

"Yes and yes. He'd never held my attention before, but I remember seeing him. He did keep showing up to class, but he put his mat well away from mine and the gal he was creeping on."

"Interesting. What does he look like?"

Niall blew out a breath. "Average height. Average build. Brown hair."

"Do you remember what color his eyes were? Skin tone?"

"He's white. Eye color, though, that's beyond my observational skills, I'm afraid."

"No worries. Did he have any unusual features, like a tattoo or a scar?"

He shook his head. "Nope. Just a boring-looking dude."

"Got it. I'll just write down 'boring-looking dude.' Is this guy the only person to have threatened you?"

"Yep," Niall confirmed.

"Do you think there's a chance he's the attacker?"

He smirked. "Honestly, he struck me as all bark and no bite. Literally."

I laughed. "No bite, gotcha. Did you tell the cops about the argument?"

"I was pretty out of it then. I honestly forgot all about it until now."

I nodded. "Tell them when you can. Thanks for talking to me, Niall. This has been incredibly helpful." I looked at my sleek black watch. It was only noon. I had plenty of time to roll over to the yoga studio.

Turning around, I slipped my notebook into my backpack. "Can I contact you if I have any more questions?"

"Of course." He put his number in my phone.

I started to roll to the door, but his voice stopped me. "Josie? Nail the attacker, okay?"

"With Dracula as my witness, I'll do my best."

Chapter Twelve

While sitting outside Out for Blood with a boring B+ blood bag and the sun on my face, I'd called the store to see how things were going. Dawk had simply said, "Busy but not so busy that you should stop saving our lives." Then he'd hung up.

Fair enough, I'd thought.

The yoga studio was behind the library, less than a ten-minute roll away. I'd driven to the hospital and Out for Blood, but the sun and fifty-degree weather were calling my name, so I wheeled myself over to Vampyasa.

The little brick building had a tasteful Valentine's Day banner hanging in its picture window and a ten-inch purple heart on the door. The heart held an announcement for a special couples yoga class on the thirteenth. Adorable.

Unfortunately, the lights were off and the door was locked. Through the glass door, I could see a small counter in front of a long room with shiny wood floors. Blankets, bolsters, and blocks filled two huge shelving units on the far wall on either side of a closed door.

I knocked, the door rattling in its frame. Nothing happened, so I knocked again. It was possible Willow was hiding behind the closed door.

Just as I was pulling out my phone to check the class schedule, movement caught my eye. Willow had emerged from the far door. She wore gorgeous purple-and-white floral leggings with a matching purple hoodie. The look of confusion on her heart-shaped face changed to a smile as she recognized me.

"Josie! What's up? Nice wheels," she said as she opened the front door.

While I'd never been to the studio, Willow and I were friendly. We were a couple of years apart, but we had several business classes together while in college. Arteria Falls being small, we'd bump into each other regularly at The Bloody Grape or other spots around town.

"Thanks, Willow! I don't think I've seen you since that party for the animal shelter." I snickered. "Remember how drunk Lynnae was?"

A melodious laugh burst from her. "Yeah I do. She kept telling that story about the pickles, the raccoon, and her great-grandmother's hairdryer. I helped you get her to the bus stop since she kept tripping over your crutch."

"Thanks again for that. Are you between classes right now?"

"Yep. Just working on some of the less glamorous aspects of business ownership."

I bobbed my head. "I know all about that."

She held the door open and motioned for me to roll inside. "How are things at the shop?"

Luckily, the door had a little threshold ramp, so I made it inside easily. My tires squealed like a ferret in a foxhole, though. The nurse from earlier would have lost her fangs.

I sighed, maybe a bit too dramatically. "Business is fine, except…well, have you heard about the attacks?"

"Oh yeah. My mom's friend Roxie knows everything that happens in this town," Willow told me. "My mom talked my ear off about it and said at least twenty times, 'I'm so glad you have brown hair.'"

I grinned. "I know Roxie too. Her gossip made its way to me as well, which is good because, as you can see…" I fluffed my hair and pointed to my eyes.

Willow grimaced. "You must be so on edge."

"Considering myself and my cousin both received hearts, 'on edge' would be putting it lightly. I slept with my crutch on the bed in case I needed a weapon."

Her face paled. "You both got hearts? That's terrible."

"Yeah, but apparently they're showing up all over town now, so it could be nothing. The attacker might be trying to confuse everyone."

Willow sat down on the floor, legs in front of her, and reached for her toes. Yoga clearly relaxed her, as she was a bit less pale when she sat back up. "Yeah, maybe now that they've attacked twice, they don't want to announce exactly who they're going after. I hope the police catch the vamp responsible soon."

"That's why I'm here."

A confused look crossed her face. "Because of the police?"

"No, because the police are overwhelmed. I can't leave this in their hands while my cousin is in danger...and me too. Remember back in college how I worked for my Grandpa Roan?"

Recognition filled her eyes. "That's right! You were always getting back to the dorms at weird hours after stakeouts. We all thought your job was so cool. I mean, the rest of us were filing papers or making grilled cheeses for humans."

I chuckled. "It wasn't that cool. Stakeouts are generally pretty boring. There were some exciting moments, though."

"I take it you're not too excited about this investigation, though?"

"You are correct. I only have one lead so far…and it brought me here."

She looked very taken aback. "Erm, here?"

"Yep. Have you heard who the two victims are yet?"

She shook her head as she went into a child's pose. "Not yet," she said, her voice bouncing off the floor.

"Maggie Dodson and Niall Haddock."

She flew up so fast that I was sure she'd pulled a muscle. Then I remembered most people don't pull or spasm muscles every three seconds like me.

"Maggie and Niall?" She looked like she was going to be sick.

"Just breathe, Willow."

She closed her eyes and took a couple of deep breaths before doing a slight back bend. "Thanks, Josie. I didn't expect *two* of my students to be victims. Wait, you don't think that I—"

I cut her off. "Fangs no. I don't think it's you."

Willow took the Buddhist principle of ahimsa, or doing no harm, very seriously. I'd once watched her spend twenty minutes trying to get a gnat out of one of the sinks in our dorm.

You might be thinking, *Why on earth would you spend twenty minutes watching someone try to save a bug, Josie?* Here's the thing: Lynnae had a crowd of biology students in our room playing the world's geekiest game about proteins and enzymes. One of her guests kept hinting at *my* proteins and enzymes, so I'd run to the bathroom to hide from him.

Back to Willow—if she turned out to be the culprit, I'd be absolutely flabbergasted.

"You had me worried for a second. What can I do to help?"

I pulled out my trusty notebook. "Willow, the only connection between the two victims I have so far is this studio. I need to research more, but so far, you're it. How often does Maggie attend classes here?"

She held up two fingers. "Twice a week. Tuesdays and Thursdays at noon." That matched what Maggie had told me. "She'd never missed a class until recently. I assumed she was sick…I didn't think…"

"I know. It's unthinkable. What about Niall?"

"He came most Mondays, Wednesdays, and Fridays to my five o'clock class."

Again, that matched what Niall said.

"So, the two never overlapped?"

She shook her head. "Nope. They both stuck to those times."

"Okay. Can you think of any students who attend both Maggie's class and Niall's class?" While the guy Niall fought with was a good suspect, I needed to know whether there were any students who might know both victims.

She bit her lip in thought. "I can't think of anyone who regularly attends both times. I have quite a few students who bounce around between classes, though, so it's possible there's a student who's been in classes with Maggie and Niall before."

"If you think of anyone, let me know, please."

"Of course. Is that all?"

I flipped back to my notes about Niall's argument. "One more thing. Niall told me he had an altercation with another student."

"Oh my fangs, that was so weird. Niall has been coming here for years. I've never seen him even remotely upset."

I asked Willow to walk me through what happened. She'd noticed the argument around the time "the dude," as Niall had called him, grabbed onto Niall's shirt. She was hesitant to put herself between them, but fortunately, another male vampire, Wyatt, pushed between them, at which point she threatened to ban them.

"Thank the Goddess that Wyatt broke them up. The last thing I need is a round of fisticuffs in my studio. I've spent years filling it with peace and tranquility."

"I'm glad you didn't have to get involved yourself. Can you remember the last thing they said to each other?"

Willow straightened her ponytail. "No, sorry. I just remember them being in each other's faces."

I was hoping she could confirm the "You better shut your mouth, or I'll shut it for you" threat against Niall. Ah well. "What is the other guy's name? Do you know where I can find him?"

"His name is Eddie. You know Arteria View?"

I raised an eyebrow. "The nursing home? What, is he 145 years old?"

With a laugh she said, "He works there, not lives there. I think he does something with activities, but that's all I know." She cringed. "They have some kind of annual dance. He invited me this year. I told him I don't socialize with students, but really it's because he's…unpleasant."

"Gotcha. Would you be able to give me a phone number or address?"

"Oh, no. I do keep records for clients who have memberships here, but those records are confidential."

I'd assumed that would be her answer. "Of course, but I had to ask. Well, I'll let you get back to your super fun administrative work. If you think of anything that could help me, let me know."

She rolled to her belly and said, "Will do," as she pushed herself into a downward dog.

"Thanks, Willow. I'll buy you a blend next time I see you at The Bloody Grape."

From between her legs, she winked and said, "Only if Lynnae tells the pickle-raccoon-hairdryer story."

Chapter Thirteen

"Then he crashed into my desk and almost knocked my monitor to the floor, but I managed to catch it just before it hit the tile. Now we only do the laser pointer in the kitchen."

I couldn't help cracking up at the image of the massive Rhodesian Ridgeback I was petting running into a desk. "Did you almost kill your dad's monitor, Mickey?"

Mickey just wagged his tail at me and rubbed his butt against my legs.

"He waits by the kitchen every night for laser pointer time," Mickey's dad, a hulking human in khaki shorts, told me. The temperature had dropped to thirty degrees in the two hours I'd been back at the store, but sure, shorts were totally appropriate. "Mickey's been so sad since the laser pointer quit working."

I gave Mickey a little pat on the butt. "Poor baby. Let's get you a new laser pointer."

Signaling for the two to follow me, I rolled to the middle of the shop. We crowded into an aisle full of less-cute dog toys, like tennis ball launchers.

I grabbed a laser pointer off the shelf. "This one is a standard laser pointer that takes batteries." I put it back and grabbed another. "Batteries are annoying though, so I recommend this laser pointer. It charges via USB. Beyond your typical red dot, this baby has different shapes for the laser, like a mouse."

"That's so cool. Mickey hates mice, so that's totally appropriate for him," Man-Who-Doesn't-Get-Cold said, but I barely heard him because Dawk popped his head around the end of the aisle, eyes wide, hair a little fluffed.

Dawk's head retreated, so I moved on. Patting a box on the middle shelf, I said, "That's a great laser pointer for you to use together, but if Mickey loves it that much, you might want to check this out. It's an automatic laser pointer. You can set it on the counter and—" I broke off as my cousin popped around the corner again, signaling at me with a sign language only he could understand. His hair had gone from mildly fluffed to 80s hair metal in the fifteen seconds he'd been gone. Uh-oh.

Mickey's dad started to turn but I cleared my throat. "Sorry! Just got a bit distracted. Anyway, you can set it on the kitchen counter and let it send the red dot all over the floor. You can even set a sched—" Dawk was now standing in the aisle with Lacey, pointing at her and then pointing at Man-Who-Doesn't-Get-Cold, "—ule. A schedule. I'm so sorry, sir. Could you excuse me? My lovely employee Lacey can take over."

I followed Dawk to the storeroom. "What's up that couldn't wait another two minutes for me to make that sale?" I lightly chided.

"Everly got a heart on her bike basket, Josie!" He ran a hand through his hair again, sending it into Einstein territory.

"Okay, Dawk. Don't freak out too much. Lots of people are getting hearts. This is her first one, right?"

He nodded as he started to pace.

"Both victims got two hearts before their attacks, so I think she's safe for now."

Dawk stopped pacing and looked at me. "Josie, you and I both got two hearts! One on the front door of the shop, and we each got another one."

I had come to that same conclusion earlier. There was no way to tell which one of us the heart on the door was meant for…or if it was for us both.

"I know. Both victims were attacked in the middle of the night while they were home alone. So I've been thinking—you should come stay with me."

He sat down on a pallet of dog food. "Last time I crashed at your place, after that 20s party you had, you banned me from staying ever again due to my 'infernal snoring.'"

"I still think Lucifer himself designed your ridiculously loud snores just to torture me, but I've got earplugs. This is more important than snores. You live alone. Let's not risk it. Unless you want to stay with your mother…or mine."

That did it. He shuddered. "Heck no. I just need to go home after work to get my stuff. I wish Everly could just come sleep at my place instead, but her dad is like…really scary."

"C'mon this will be way better than that. It will be just like our childhood sleepovers. We can rent *Jumanji* and *The Sandlot*!"

"I'll bring those blood and dark chocolate bars we used to binge as kids."

"Right…'used to binge as kids.' I definitely don't still do that every Saturday night."

"So, are we piling sleeping bags on the floor and building a fort around them?"

I laughed at my cousin as he handed me a blood-chocolate bar. "Only if we're pulling my mattress out here first. I'm pretty sure if I sleep on the floor, my body will just refuse to function tomorrow. You'll have to run the store all by yourself."

"On a Sunday? No, thanks," he said as he walked to the kitchen to get us a couple of wine glasses.

I'd left Zippy in my room and switched to the crutch. I tapped over to the couch, ready to make a nest and relax my ailing body. Threats to oneself and one's family are powerful motivation, but my body wasn't enjoying the extra exertion.

Matilda's head was perched on top of Dawk's duffel bag, her body stretched out on a throw pillow.

"Well, look at you. Did you find yourself a new place to sleep?" Her little tail wagged. "Unfortunately, I'm going to have to move you and this duffel bag, 'cause I desperately need to lay down."

I slowly scooted the bag out from under her. She sat up on the throw pillow, huffed at me, and took off for my bedroom.

"Ah, c'mon, Matilda! It's snuggle time." No response. "Boo."

Dawk set two glasses on the coffee table and popped open the blood-wine blend. "She'll be back. It's too cold for her to stay away."

Matilda proved him right once I got both my heating pads turned on and the third blanket spread over me. It's like she could smell the heating pads…although, maybe she could, what did I know?

She popped her head around the corner of the couch, her fluffy eyebrows bouncing. Low-crawling across the ground, as if we couldn't see her, she made her way toward the middle of the couch.

"Get up here, girl." Jumping up, she spun around on me a few times and then plopped, instantly asleep.

Sitting down in one of the chairs across from me, Dawk laughed at her antics. "I wish I could fall asleep that quickly. I barely slept at all last night."

"Well, you'll be safe here tonight. Three vampires and a dog? The attacker won't risk it."

He sighed. "Yeah, I'm sure you're right. Where's Lynnae?"

A grin spread across my face. "She's having a drink with my physical therapist."

"Wow, really? How did that happen?"

"Remember the guy she kept staring at during Grandpa Roan's century party a few months back?"

His eyes lit up in recognition. "Oh yeah! I'd forgotten about that."

"Before the party ended, she approached him, and they got to talking."

"I didn't realize he was your physical therapist." My cousin put his foot on the coffee table. "Maybe he can help me with a bit of Achilles tendinitis."

"Your Achilles tendon is hurting? I didn't realize. Are you okay to be walking around the shop all day?"

He chuckled. "Yep, I'm fine. It's really only been acting up while I'm playing soccer. I was talking to some of the guys about it after practice last week. They told me how to tape it, so I'm okay. It's nothing like…" Dawk gestured to me as he trailed off.

I sat up a bit, wrapping an arm around Matilda to steady her. "Dawk, just because I have a whole bag of health issues doesn't mean I don't want to know when something is going on with you. Don't keep quiet because of my issues."

He nodded but looked uncomfortable. "Back to Lynnae, the party was months ago, she doesn't usually move so slow."

I giggled. "I know, right? At first, she was saying it was too awkward to date my PT, but finally, she told me she 'doesn't want to fang this up like all the others.'"

"Aww. How cute. Lynnae's caught the love bug, just in time for Valentine's Day."

"Definitely. It seems like everyone is coupling up. What are you and Everly doing for Valentine's Day? You know, once you recover from helping at the bakery all night on the thirteenth."

He gave me an irritated look. "I'm *so* looking forward to that, by the way."

"What?" I gasped. "You aren't excited to spend all night locked in a bakery, covered in flour and icing?"

"Mm-hmm. So excited. Back to your question, I'm planning on making a special blend, stealing some baked goods from Isa's, and doing a candlelit dinner at my place. Though I guess I'll have to come back here to sleep after."

"You guess? You mean you're so lucky to come back here to sleep. Speaking of, let's get this party started."

I grabbed the remote off the coffee table. "Jumanji and hairy Robin Williams, here we come."

Chapter Fourteen

Sunday morning had come way too soon. Even after having taken all my medicine and having sprawled out on my heated mattress pad all night, my body hadn't recovered from all the recent activity.

After drinking a gallon of coffee and basically taking a bath in Bengay, I'd felt a little like a vampire instead of a stoned sloth. I'd put a thin back brace on under my blood-red, bell-sleeve top to hopefully keep the pain down.

Dawk was supposed to take Matilda to the store when ten o'clock rolled around, so I'd only had to load Zippy into the van.

By a quarter after eight, I was in the lobby of Arteria View, where a woman with a severe bob told me Eddie had the day off.

"I seem to have misplaced his phone number, do you think you could…" I trailed off as her face pinched.

"Of course I can't give you his phone number. Do I look like a phone book? I'm very busy, so please—" She'd stopped talking then, instead fluttering her hand toward the door.

Not ready to give up, I circled the property. It was a cold morning, about twenty degrees, but my thick coat allowed me to enjoy the roll around the expansive building. The birds were chirping in the pine trees that surrounded the property, and the sun was shining. Even when it's cold as Dracula's heart in Colorado, the sun still shines—most days.

Window after window of residential rooms lined the long building, but when I got to the back, I found huge windows with a view into a drab dining room. Seniors were spread out around round tables, eating a boring-looking breakfast. A few of them waved to me, and I enthusiastically waved back.

Next to the dining room, I found a pile of boxes near an industrial door, which was propped open just a tad. Clanking and sizzling noises floated out to me, confirming that this was the kitchen.

Just as I was debating opening the door to let myself in, a hoarse voice said, "I'm going on break." The door flew open before I could move Zippy out of the way.

SMACK. Right into my wheel.

"What the? Oh fangs, I'm sorry," the man said.

I waved him off once I parked Zippy a few feet back. "Don't worry about it. It was a dumb place for me to be."

He let the door close and leaned on the wall. Despite the chill, he didn't wear a coat, just a dirty apron. Maybe his scraggly beard kept him warm. "Why are you back here? The entrance is 'round front."

I watched the man pull a pack of cigarettes and a lighter out of his pocket, trying to determine how best to get information out of him. He pushed his long hair out of his face and lit a cigarette.

Deciding a direct approach would be best, I dove right in. "I'll be honest with you. I'm looking for some information and the front desk wasn't helpful."

He laughed but it turned into a cough. "Not surprised. They're a bit *surly* at the desk. What kind of information are you looking for?"

"I'm investigating a private matter. Do you know Eddie? I think he does activities here?"

An O of smoke floated toward me. "Yep. He's the worst. Even surlier than the gals up front. He's so weird too."

"Weird how?"

"He creeps out some of the women who work here. Makes weird comments. And he's really into bugs."

I curled my lip. "Bugs?"

"Yep. Bugs. Talks about them all the time and has a huge collection at home."

Bile rose up my throat just thinking about a bug collection. "Speaking of his home…do you know where he lives?"

The man nodded, blowing smoke out of his nose. Before he could tell me, someone opened the door to throw an empty box onto the teetering pile.

My new informant waved me further away from the door. He put out the cigarette with his shoe and leaned toward me.

"You know the little neighborhood right behind city hall?"

"Of course—Arteria Falls' first houses."

He nodded. "Eddie brags about living there all the time. So annoying. It's not even his house—it's his mom's. My parents live there too, but I don't tell the whole world."

"Any idea which house is theirs?"

He smiled, revealing tar-stained teeth. "It's the one with all the flamingos on Newberry Street. You can't miss it."

A breeze whipped along the building, and his nostrils flared. "Ugh, what's that smell? It's like a mint that stings your nostrils."

Really? Cigarette-Man, who smelled like cigarettes, was offended by the Bengay I'd slathered over every inch of skin I could reach?

"It's my new perfume." I tossed my hair over my shoulder with a flair. "Essence of stinging mint. Thanks for your help."

On that note, Zippy and I went flamingo hunting.

"All the flamingos" had been a vast understatement. This yard was a breeding ground for plastic and ceramic flamingos. Plastic flamingos on wires were stuck in the ground every few feet, some wearing little sweaters, others left bare. A stone bird bath was held up by a flamingo sculpture. Flamingo figurines sat on the porch railing. Small flamingo lights hung around the front door. Garden gnomes riding—you guessed it—flamingos sat at the base of the porch stairs.

As you can imagine, the stairs weren't wheelchair friendly, so I grabbed my cane and carefully made my way up them. I'd learned the hard way that anything over five stairs was likely to cause a back spasm, but thankfully, this was only four stairs.

I made it to the top and took a deep breath, feeling like I'd reached the summit of a mountain. With a smile plastered on my face, I rang the flamingo-encased doorbell. That's right, the little doorbell was set in the middle of a ceramic flamingo.

A short vampire in what looked like a homemade Valentine's Day sweatshirt answered the door. She looked surprised to see me, but she recovered quickly. Her round face was bright as she said, "Well, hello, dear. How can I help you?" She looked down at my cane, and her eyes lit up. "Oh my fangs! I love your cane. That's my favorite color."

I'll give you one guess as to the color of the cane I'd grabbed that morning. Did you guess pink?

I tightened my grip on the cane, nervous she'd steal it and stick a flamingo on top. "I'm so glad you like it! This is my favorite cane. My name is Josie."

I stuck my hand out, and she shook it vigorously.

"I'm Judith."

"Nice to meet you! I was wondering if Eddie is here?"

Her brow furrowed in confusion. "Eddie?" She looked at me closely, taking in my long hair and curvy figure. "You're here for Eddie?"

If I had to guess, I'd say lady callers didn't come to the door for Eddie often.

"Yes, I need to speak with him."

"About…"

I smiled, trying to put her at ease. "Just a few questions about something that happened during a yoga class."

"Oh. I didn't know something happened at yoga. Were you there?"

I shook my head. "No. I know the owner, though. I'm an investigator."

"*Investigator?*" Judith's shoulders tensed. "No, no. Eddie isn't here. Sorry."

Next thing I knew, a beautiful, but weird, wreath covered in fluffy, pink hearts and a hand-painted flamingo was flying at my face as she closed the door.

Thankful as ever for my combat boots, I blocked the door with my foot, holding the door frame for support. I did not want to fall over in flamingo territory. They might come to life and peck my eyes out.

"Judith, you have every right to close the door, and I'm sorry to be so rude, but I know Eddie is off today. Can you tell me where he is?"

She cracked the door, her face pinched. "I have nothing further to—"

"MA! Have you seen Terry? I put him on the bed, but now I can't find him."

Her face fell as I called out, "Eddie?"

"Ma. Is that someone for me?" The voice, whiny and impatient, got closer. "Are you going to move or what?"

Judith stepped back, scowling at me instead of her rude son.

Eddie appeared in all his unshaven and, it quickly became apparent, unwashed glory. He looked me up and down, stopping way too long on my chest, before giving me a *look*.

An unwelcome look.

I scowled at him just a bit, but his beady brown eyes didn't pick up on it.

"How can I help you today, little lady?"

Little lady is one of my least favorite misogynistic names for women. I was about to show this guy how *not little* I was by sticking my ever-so-useful combat boot where he'd never mistake it for *little*.

He was *little* himself. Just like his mom, he was about an inch shorter than me.

"My name is Josie. I'm hoping you can help me. I have just a few questions about an incident at Vampyasa about a month ago."

With a sleazy grin, he said, "I'm sure I can help you. Why don't we discuss this in my room?"

My stomach tightened. I did not want to go to this creep's room. He could be the attacker, but even if he wasn't, he screamed *creeper*.

"Could we perhaps speak on the porch?"

"Are you crazy? It's cold out there."

Not waiting for a reply, he turned and walked into the house.

With a sigh, I stepped inside, glad to have my cane in case I needed an impromptu weapon.

Y'all, if the outside of this house was a festival of flamingos, the inside was the epicenter of flamingo activity on earth. There were more flamingos in the house than there were real flamingos on the whole planet. Throw pillows, blankets, wall hangings, bunting, figurines, and so much more.

I'm pretty sure an interior designer would have a heart attack in here.

Me? My mouth dropped open a little, but I managed to keep it together as I followed Eddie through the living room and into a hallway.

Ignoring the flamingo horror show, the house was nice. Judith kept it up well—I'm assuming Eddie was no help. The wood floors gleamed. No dust was in sight.

Eddie's baggy basketball shorts swished as he led me down the hall. We passed a guest room that was mercifully decorated with floral decor, a spacious bathroom, and a craft room that would make my grandmother blush green with envy. White shelves covered every wall, except one, where a long table was covered with in-progress Valentine's crafts. The room was meticulously organized and clearly well-loved.

"It's through here." Eddie's voice pulled me away from the craft room.

A poster about the types of spiders greeted us when we reached his door. Cigarette-Man had been right about Eddie's bug love.

I almost tripped as I stepped through the doorway, but my cane caught me. The bug love was much more than a mere poster. Eddie clearly inherited his mother's obsessive focus on an obscure creature…only Eddie's collection was alive.

Spiders. Spiders everywhere. Shelves and shelves of terrariums.

Orange spiders, black spiders, furry spiders, and a whole ensemble of creepy crawlers staring at me through their many, many eyes.

My fangs almost snapped down of their own accord, determined to show these little buggers who was boss, but I contained them.

"Have a seat," Eddie said, gesturing to the bed.

It was the only place to sit in the whole room. I was so tempted to take the pressure off my legs, but by that point, I was sure Terry, who Eddie said had gone missing on the bed, was not a harmless bunny rabbit.

"Umm, that's okay. I'll stand."

He shrugged and fell back on the bed. "Don't mind if I do then. So you have questions about yoga?"

"Yes, about the confrontation that occurred a month ago or so."

"That guy has a serious stake up his butt. I don't know what his problem was. Why do you care?"

"I'm an investigator." I reached into my jacket pocket to grab my PI license.

"Nice picture," Eddie said with a wink. Eww.

Ignoring that comment, I told him, "I'm looking into a matter involving Niall, the man you argued with."

"Is that his name? Whatever your investigating's got nothing to do with me."

"I'm just checking all the boxes here. Getting a feel for any incidents surrounding him."

He snorted. "Multiple incidents, huh? Not surprised. I hope this matter you mentioned involved him getting handed his fangs."

Eddie clearly held some aggression toward Niall still. But how much aggression? "Why would you say that?"

"The guy needs to learn to keep to himself. He got in my business for nothing."

I raised an eyebrow. "For nothing? How did the altercation begin?"

"He'd been giving me angry looks all through class. At the end, he made a *noise* at me. I'd had enough, so I got in his face. He seemed to have a problem with where I put my eyes, which is none of his business. I'll look at whoever I want."

Did this guy hear himself? Did he think I would be on his side?

"Uh-huh. So, you got in his face. Did it turn physical?"

"Naw. Some blond dude got between us. Then Willow threatened to kick us out. The yoga really helps a groin injury I have, so I decided to back off." I hoped that injury was from someone nailing his groin with a nice kick. "Otherwise, I would have put that guy in his place."

Yeah, let me just say that my money was on Niall in that fight.

"Have you seen him again?"

"Yep. Several times."

"Any further encounters between you?"

"Nope, but his smug little grin makes me want to smother him with my yoga mat."

Interesting. Was that all manly-man posturing, or had Eddie acted on his threat?

"Have you ever seen Niall outside of yoga?"

"No, why?"

I waved off his question. "Just curious. Do you ever go to yoga during the day?"

"Just after work."

I looked around the room, trying to think of a way to get Eddie to tell me about his life. "These spiders are impressive. Do you work with spiders professionally?"

A fire lit in Eddie's eyes. "That would be amazing. I've tried to find somewhere in the vamp world where I could work with spiders, but I haven't found anything. I just work over at Arteria View now."

"Oh! My friend's great-grandmother lives there." Lie. "I love visiting her there."

He rubbed his stubble. "It's okay. I do activities, so I just have to show up and play with the old folks."

"Play with them?" I asked.

"Yep. It's like preschool. Read to them. Do some stretching. Decorate cookies. Make cards or other crafts."

I gave him a genuine smile. "That sounds like fun."

"I guess."

I shifted, transferring my weight to the opposite leg. My knees were screaming from standing too long. "At least you don't have to work nights. I imagine the nursing home needs some staff to work at night."

Eddie bobbed his head. "Yeah, they need caregivers on all night. Some janitors too. I only work during the day." He stood, his smarmy smile back. "I have plenty of nights free."

Ugh. My questions about his life seemed to be giving him the wrong impression, but I decided to lean into it. "That's cool. What kind of stuff do you do at night?"

"Other than take care of these little guys," his gaze trailed across the terrariums, "I play a couple of tabletop games with my friends."

"How fun! My friends and I play a few board games. Do you guys ever hang out near the college? I know they have game tournaments sometimes."

If Eddie was the attacker, he had to have a connection to Maggie, who seemed to only go to yoga and campus.

"One of my friends lives nearby, but I don't really go on campus. We haven't done the tournaments in years." He took a step closer. "Do you?"

"Two of my good friends are researchers, so I stop by their lab regularly, but I don't do the game tournaments." I moved my cane a bit in front of me, attempting to redistribute the pressure in my lower body, but unfortunately, the move required me to bend forward a bit. Eddie took that the wrong way.

"Well, *Josie*," I cringed a bit as he said my name with an oily smugness, "maybe sometime we could play a game."

Electricity shot up my leg, my poor limb struggling to keep me up. I looked down and found a huge spider slowly ambulating up my cane.

My scream echoed around the room as I dropped the cane and backed into the door, adrenaline pushing the pain away.

"Oh that's just Terry, my tarantula. He's harmle—"

Something slammed into the door, pitching me forward. Judith hustled into the room holding a rolling pin just as I fell into Eddie's arms. I had a half second to note that he really, really needed a shower before his mom pushed between us.

Steadying me, she looked me over. "What happened?" She looked at her son. "Give Josie her cane back."

"MA! Calm down. Terry just crawled onto her cane and freaked her out." Eddie handed over my cane. "He ran off again, though."

My heart was still racing, but I'd calmed down enough to wonder what Judith thought was happening. Had she been standing around with a rolling pin in case I hurt her son? But when she ran into the room, she wasn't concerned about Eddie at all. She'd been concerned about me. Maybe she knew her son was a creep.

It didn't matter. I just needed to get out of that flamingo-arachnid jungle.

After a deep breath, I announced that I was late for a meeting and backed out of the room, praying to the Goddess that I didn't put my cane on Terry-the-Tarantula.

Chapter Fifteen

"Colleen?"

A messy red bun popped up from a study carrel. "This is a *quiet* study room," the young woman attached to the bun told me.

I looked around. "No one else is in here."

"Yes, but *I'm* in here because *I* want quiet."

No wonder Maggie had wished me "good luck and good fangs" after texting me that Colleen frequented this bland study room tucked in a dingy corner of the library.

I smiled at the uptight vampire who was squeezing her pen so hard I thought it would burst. "Sorry, but I really need to speak with you. That is, if you're Colleen?"

She set her pen down and slammed her textbook shut. "Fine. Make this quick. I have a test next Tuesday."

Next Tuesday? As in nine days from now? This vamp really needed to unclench.

"Thanks *so* much," I said in a syrupy sweet voice. "I'll try to be quick. You're friends with Maggie Dodson, right?"

"HA!" She threw her head back and let out a villainous laugh, something out of a Disney movie. "Friends? Yeah, right. More like mortal enemies."

Yep, she was definitely a Disney villain.

"Hmm, I guess I got my wires crossed somewhere." I knew they weren't friends but I'd wanted to see her reaction.

"Ya think? Who even are you?"

I rolled Zippy closer and held out a hand. "Josie Wixx, private investigator extraordinaire." I flourished my other hand through the air and gave a little bow, hand still held out.

"I'd prefer not to touch you. Nothing personal." I noted what could not be called a travel-sized bottle of hand sanitizer next to a pack of disinfectant wipes on the desk. "A PI, huh? Is Maggie on the run from her family or something? Were you sent to bring her back to whatever Podunk vampire hole she crawled out of?"

"Umm." My mind was on pause, the tape stuck, looping Colleen's words.

"You aren't a very good PI, are you? What kind of response is 'umm'? Unless…I get it now. This is your first case."

That snapped me back to reality. "Excuse me. I don't know what your deal is, but this is nowhere near my first case. Your words just shocked me a bit. I haven't heard anything so rude since my Great-Aunt Ginnie got thrown out of bingo for calling the organizer a knobby-kneed, dopehead charlatan. Now, if you're done, we can move things forward."

Her green eyes widened in shock for a few moments before a snarky grin appeared. "I like you. No one's been that forward with me in ages." She flicked her wrist. "Ask me your questions."

As I pulled out my notebook, I got straight to the point. "You clearly dislike Maggie. Why?"

"She thinks she knows everything but she's not even that smart. I honestly have no idea how she gets such good grades. Sometimes I think the professors pity her because she has, like, no friends."

Right. That was the only possible explanation for someone beating out Colleen.

"So," I said, "that's it?"

Colleen twirled a strand of hair that'd freed itself from her bun—no doubt trying to make a break from all the pretentiousness. "No, it's complicated, though. She's just always stealing my ideas, trying to get ahead of me."

"Gotcha. Is Maggie generally disliked then? She sounds awful."

"No! She has everyone wrapped around her fangs." Colleen threw her hands up. "I don't understand it at all."

I let my mouth drop open a little. "Really? Strange. You can't think of anyone else who has an issue with her?"

"Wait, why? Did something happen?"

"I really can't say." No way was I going to tell Colleen what happened. Not only was she still a suspect, but I'm sure she would tell the whole Anthropology Department and beyond.

Her eyes glinted. "Oh my fangs, something happened." She gasped. "That's why Maggie was gone this week! I thought she was sick or something. Tell me everything."

I crossed my arms. "As I said, I can't talk about it." Letting my arms drop to my wheels, I said, "If you can't help, I'll just have to find someone more capable—"

She scoffed. "I never said I couldn't help."

Bingo. I'd hit her competitiveness right on the head.

"Well, then, why don't *you* tell *me* everything?"

"If something really did happen to Maggie, you need to find the weirdo who watches her."

My heart skipped a beat. "Someone watches her?"

"Yep. Maggie has no idea. You know the pavilion between here and the rec center?"

"With all the metal picnic tables?"

"That's the one. Maggie eats lunch there a few days a week, even when it's absolutely freezing outside. She's almost always alone, except when Shauna—an admin in the department—eats with her." Colleen rolled her eyes, like it was ridiculous that Maggie would be so friendly with department staff. "I pass by on my way to the student union. There's this guy who watches her from over by the rec center."

"Every time Maggie is there?"

She shook her head, another strand of hair falling. "No, just most days."

"What does he look like?"

Without missing a beat she said, "Tall, sandy-blond hair, pale, clean-shaven. Boring khakis and polos. Carries a duffel bag."

"I wish all my interviewees were as observant as you."

Haughtiness radiated from her as she said, "I'm sure you do."

Wow. "Anything else you remember about him, or is there anyone else you can think of?"

"Nope."

"Okay. Just a couple more questions. Do you ever go to Vampyasa?"

She grabbed her stomach. "Just the thought of doing yoga makes me want to vomit. All that inner peace and relaxation? Eww."

I chuckled, not surprised she wasn't a yogi. "Do you know anyone who works at First Blood?"

"The blood supplier? Noooo?" She stretched the word out, clearly confused and hoping I would explain my question.

No such luck for her. I released my brakes. "Thanks, Colleen. Good luck on your test."

"I don't need luck, but thanks anyway."

She turned back to her carrel, grabbing her hand sanitizer even though we hadn't touched.

As I rolled out of the library, my thoughts whirled. Who was this stranger watching Maggie? If Colleen was right, Maggie didn't even know he watched her, so how would I find him?

"Hey, bestie! Why are you working on Sunday *again*?"

Lynnae looked up from her microscope. "One second, Jos." She slid her laptop across the sleek metal table she stood at and typed as if the keyboard owed her money. My roomie got so excited about her research that she typed a little too enthusiastically sometimes. Calder, who ran the lab, had to have IT replace her keyboard after a particularly exciting research find last year.

"Okay," she said, clapping her hands. "What are you doing here?"

"Investigating, of course. I was at the library. I figured you'd be here since you were droning on about work when you got home last night."

She nodded. "You know me so well. I can't resist the call of the lab."

I pulled off my gloves and rubbed my fingers together. "You could find a hobby like a normal person."

"Cha. I make blood blends—that's a hobby."

I nodded. "Sure, but you only do that in the middle of the night when you can't sleep."

"It still counts!" she insisted.

Laughing, I rolled closer to her. "I know, I'm just teasing you. The Goddess knows I'm not any better. Here I am, out digging for clues."

Her eyebrows raised. "Aren't you supposed to be at the store?"

"Dawk seems to think our lives are more important. He won't care if I'm late."

"Touché. Find any clues?"

I sighed. "Kinda?" I filled her in on my Sunday sleuthing. "So, Eddie doesn't seem to have a connection to Maggie, and Colleen doesn't have a connection to Niall."

"Okay, so you have one suspect per victim, but no way to connect the suspects to the other victim?"

"Exactly," I said, lightly banging my fist on my thigh. "I think I can rule Colleen out, but Eddie? I'm not so sure."

"Yeah, Eddie sounds pretty creepy. I wouldn't rule him out either. Maybe he randomly hit on Maggie somewhere and she rejected him. But why rule out Colleen? She could be lying, or she could have some unknown connection to Niall."

Nodding, I said, "You're right, but Colleen wouldn't shake my hand. She had a tank of hand sanitizer with her."

Lynnae's eyes widened as she made the connection. "She's a germaphobe."

"Yep. No way is she biting people. She'd have to have someone else do it, but that doesn't feel right to me. This whole thing is personal. The biting vamp is doing their own dirty work, not someone else's."

"Makes sense." She made an X in the air. "Colleen is no longer a suspect. But the creepy watcher she mentioned? Totally a suspect. Could it be Eddie?"

I shook my head. "No. He's super creepy, but the description doesn't fit. Eddie is short and definitely not clean-shaven."

Lynnae tapped her fingers on the table. "Maybe Maggie's stalker doesn't have anything to do with this. You said Eddie does crafts with the seniors? How morbid would it be if he had them make the hearts?"

"Oh my stars, that would be quite audacious. I could see it, though. He's cocky enough to think no one would make the connection. His mom also has an impressive craft room. He could have made the hearts there."

I pulled out my notebook and made a suspect list:

Eddie-of-the-Spiders

Strange-Stalker-Man

"What's your next move?" Lynnae asked.

"Call Maggie to see if she knows anyone that fits Strange-Stalker-Man's description." I checked my watch. "The boutique just opened a little bit ago, so I should probably go sell some luxury, faux-sherpa-lined snow boots for cold-pawed canine companions across Arteria Falls."

With a wry smile, she said, "Doing the Goddess' work."

"Indeed."

Chapter Sixteen

The late-afternoon light reflected off tiny snowflakes as they blew past the shop's floor-to-ceiling front windows. The store was empty, so I'd grabbed Reginald and parked my chair at the front of the store. "Look, Reggie. It's snowing!"

Meow

"Don't worry about Matilda. She's sleeping in my office. It's just you and me."

Meow

I pulled him closer, needing all the comfort I could get. Matilda was done with my snuggles—I'd latched onto her for twenty minutes during my break earlier—so I'd forced the cat to submit to snuzzling.

You might be thinking, *Josie, snuzzling isn't a word!* Next time you snuggle up to a cat, a dog, or a muscular man with gorgeous wavy, brown hair and an adorable dimple and you nuzzle into their neck, that's snuzzling.

The store was stocked, the floor was swept, so I watched vampires and humans stroll down Vein Street, doing their shopping or getting a glass of wine.

We'd be closing soon. It was dark by five o'clock, and especially with the snow, customers would be few and far between.

"Reggie," I said as I adjusted his Valentine's Day bow tie, "who do you think the attacker is?"

Maggie had been clueless about Strange-Stalker-Man. She didn't know anyone who fit his description, nor did she realize some guy had been watching her eat lunch. I felt bad adding to the stress she was under, but she needed to know about him. She was going back to her classes the next day, so I told her to keep an eye out for him and be extra cautious.

Before Reggie could answer me, the door dinged.

"Welcome to Matilda's VamPets!" I called out on autopilot.

"Hey, there," a man in a huge puffy coat and a beanie said.

"Oh! You're back! My old Fun for Fangs buddy. Do you need something else for...wait, don't tell me..." I trailed off, trying to remember his cat's name. After a second, I triumphantly declared her name to be "Sally!" I had no idea what his name was, but I remembered the cat. Priorities, right?

He laughed. "You got it. It turns out Sally is a picky eater. I need some different cat food."

Keeping my furry friend on my lap, I rolled over to our cat food aisle. We kept a selection of canned foods on the sales floor, but all bags stayed in the storeroom. Dawk was currently in the back tossing around said bags, trying to forget he was a target in a sick Valentine's Day vendetta.

I reviewed the options with the customer, suggesting he take a few different options home. When his arms were full, we headed to the register.

"I hope Sally takes to one of these. Sometimes it just takes time for a cat to adjust to a new home. Give her some space. She'll come around."

"I hope you're right," he said. "Are you guys closing soon? It's quiet in here."

I rolled behind the counter as he plunked the cans down. "Yep! It's about quitting time."

Reginald gave me a superbly offended look when I set him down on Matilda's under-counter bed. Ah well, he'd get over it.

"Any plans for the evening?" Puffy-Coat asked. Don't worry, he wasn't Eddie. It was clear the man was just making conversation, not hitting on me.

I started bagging the cans. "My cousin—he works here too, you might have seen him the other day—we're having a sleepover!"

The man chuckled as he adjusted his beanie. "I haven't had one of those in decades."

"We hadn't either before last night, but circumstances called for it."

He eyed my hair before checking my eyes. "Oh," he said. "Be safe out there."

"Always. That'll be $30.13."

A minute later, he was on his way to the door when another ding sounded. I rolled back out to the sales floor, ready to call out my standard greeting, but it fell from my mouth as the new arrival slammed into Puffy-Coat's shoulder.

"Watch it!" the new man said.

Puffy-Coat stopped in his tracks, jaw slack.

Red-faced, steam floating from his ears, the newcomer approached me. "Where's Dawk!?"

"Erm, hello to you, too, sir. Is there something I can help you with?"

"Did you not hear me? I'm not here to shop at this ridiculous store. I'm here for Dawk. Where is he?" The man's light-blond hair was sticking up in several directions, like the strands were trying to get away from his ire.

Puffy-Coat continued to just watch, not having moved a muscle, probably making sure the new arrival wasn't about to get violent with me.

"I'll see if he's available. Can I get your name?"

He crossed his arms, his pale blue eyes narrowing. "Just get him."

I crossed my arms too. "Your name, sir."

Fists clenching, he said, "Jack."

I rolled backward to the storeroom door, not wanting to take my eyes off Jack.

Dawk was grabbing another forty-pound dog food bag, his wireless earbuds in place.

After calling out twice to no avail, I wheeled over to poke him in the side.

Jumping a few inches, he almost dropped the bag. "You scared me. What's up?"

"There's a very angry, very unpleasant man here to see you. Name's Jack. Looks like he could be our uncle. I'm *more than happy* to tell him to fang off."

My cousin's face fell. "Ugh. That's Everly's dad."

I now understood why Dawk had called her dad "really scary."

"You want to see him, or shall I give him the boot?" I raised my foot and kicked it out.

With a long, drawn-out sigh, he said, "No. I'll go talk to him."

Puffy-Coat was gone when we got back to the sales floor. Only Jack and his attitude remained.

Not willing to let my cousin deal with him alone, I parked about a foot away from Dawk, next to a display of pastel poop bags.

Jack pushed his way into Dawk's personal space. "You need to leave my daughter alone."

My cousin leaned back. "Jack, where is this coming from?"

"You're putting her in danger. She just told me you got several of these hearts that are going around. Being around her will put her in harm's way."

"Well, sir, lots of people have received hearts, and we don't know—"

Jack cut him off, slicing his hand through the air. "Save it. The bottom line here is—"

That was my cue to interrupt. "Umm, *so sorry* to interrupt here, but Everly received a heart, didn't she?"

The man scoffed. "Yeah, just one. From what I've heard, the two vamps that got attacked have lighter hair than hers."

He wasn't wrong. Everly's hair was darker than her father's, more of a dirty blond. I hadn't thought much about that yet. Was it a coincidence that Maggie and Niall have such similar hair shades? Maybe all blonds were targets? Or was the attacker spreading so many hearts just to confuse the police and town residents?

Jack's next words to Dawk broke through my thoughts. "How do we know her heart wasn't meant for you? Maybe the attacker knows she's dating you."

Hmm. That seemed far-fetched to me, but if it was true, then I couldn't resist pointing out the obvious.

"Let's entertain that possibility, Jack. If hearts are being left for people connected to the next intended victims, how do you know it isn't you? Your eyes and hair are almost a perfect match for ours." I pointed between me and Dawk. (Which was weird, by the way. I'd have to rag on Dawk later about dating someone whose father looked like him.)

Everly's father did not like my idea. Ignoring me, he put his nose about half a centimeter from Dawk's. "Just stay away."

With that, he turned on his heel, knocking over a few dog toothbrushes, and rushed out of the shop.

"Holy fangs on a fly. What was that?" I asked.

My cousin slumped against the counter. "I don't know. Do you think he's right? Am I putting her in danger?"

Putting all the certainty I could muster behind my words, I said, "No. I do not think you are putting her in danger. Look, leaving hearts for anyone other than the intended victim is not the attacker's modus operandi. I think Jack just took too many steroids."

A quick laugh burst from Dawk. "He really does seem like he's on steroids. I thought we'd been making progress. The last few times I picked Everly up, Jack seemed less annoyed by me. Guess I was wrong. He's probably using this whole heart thing as an excuse to push me away."

"I think you're right." I rolled toward the front of the boutique and grabbed a squeaky toy shaped like a rose with little XOs on the petals. "Here. This is your new stress toy. Squeeze away."

Smiling, he took it. "You're such a weird boss."

"That's the best compliment I've had all month."

Chapter Seventeen

"My stars, it's cold out there." Shivering, I rubbed my arms over my coat sleeves as Dawk pushed my chair into the house. Matilda was already on the couch, digging in the blankets, clearly as desperate to warm up as I was.

"I'm going to need to pull out my fleece-lined-leggings layer if it gets any colder."

Twenty degrees, the current temperature, was my limit. Below that…no, thank you. My body couldn't handle it. I'd stay at home or grudgingly wear twelve layers.

"Hey there, roommate and temporary roommate."

"Lynnae!" I shouted across the house. "You're home, and you're in the kitchen!"

She carefully clipped up her gorgeous twist out before sticking her tongue out at me. "I decided you might be right. Hobbies should be an important part of life. So I'm making a blood blend at an appropriate time of day instead of the middle of the night."

I clapped. "Yay!" I pulled off my coat and rolled forward, my cousin just behind.

"Any alcohol in this blend you're making?" he asked.

"Nope, but I've got a bottle of straight Merlot you can drink."

"Thank the Goddess. I'm in desperate need."

Dawk set himself up with a glass of wine while I transferred from my wheelchair to a dining chair.

"What's going in your blend, bestie?" I asked.

She pointed at the ingredients in front of her. "Seaweed to add a bit of umami, fresh lime juice, a pinch of cayenne." She paused and pointed at a steaming mug of tea. "I'm basing it off the seaweed salad humans eat, so I wanted to add ginger too, but since we don't tolerate it well, I've got ginger tea."

"Genius," I commended her.

"I skipped the salt humans use, for obvious reasons."

Blood is salty. Like super salty. That's one of the reasons blends are so nice—you can tone down certain flavors, like salt, but play into others, like iron.

After a couple hours of sipping on Lynnae's blend—which was phenomenal—while watching *Clueless*—also phenomenal—we went to bed.

Dreaming of short yellow skirts and loud parties in the Valley, I dozed happily, Matilda at my feet.

Until she started barking up a storm.

I sat up so fast that I pulled a muscle in the back of my head. "Oww! Matilda, what gives?" I called to her. Adrenaline sang in my veins, causing my fangs to snap out.

She ran from the room, still barking. *Rawr! Rawr! Rawr! Rawr! Rawr!*

I found her in the living room, jumping at a window that led to our backyard. Dawk had been sleeping and snoring on the floor, so her barks had instantly woken him.

"What the fangs?"

"I don't know," I told him tapping my crutch beside me as I approached the window. "Matilda!"

Rawr! Rawr! Rawr! Rawr! Rawr!

"She never does this," I told Dawk.

My cousin turned on his phone flashlight and directed the beam to the window.

"Do you see anything?" I asked him.

He shook his head. "No."

I sighed. "Same."

Lynnae's slippers scratched across the floor. "What is going on?"

"We don't know. Something set Matilda off." Something or someone? Could the attacker have been out there?

Matilda ran to the front door, her barks replaced by growls. Dawk followed her, moving to open the door.

"Don't go out there! Only horror movie damsels chase noises outside," my roommate pleaded.

Dawk let out a little growl of his own. "Fine. It could be nothing, but you're right, it would be stupid to go out there, just in case it's this bloodsucking jerk attacking people."

We all plopped on the couch.

"Let's all take some deep breaths together," I suggested. Deep breaths—my go-to calming aid.

"Good idea, Josie," Lynnae said. "Let's do it."

The three of us synced our breaths, slowly pulling air in and out. My heart had been beating like a bat's wings, so I needed the zen moment myself. My fangs retreated as I breathed.

Matilda followed our lead and calmed her veins, jumping on the couch and almost instantly falling asleep. Goddess, I wished I was a dog.

When we were done, my cousin looked at me. "Do you think that was the attacker?"

Shrugging, I said, "No clue. It could have been a raccoon or just the wind."

"You've got to solve this, Jos," he said.

"I know!" I snapped. "Sorry...I'm just really feeling the pressure." I grabbed onto my long locks and twisted the hair around my fingers. "I don't know what to do next."

"Well, I do." My roomie grabbed the half-empty bottle of Merlot. "We drink."

Chapter Eighteen

O ur bungalow was quiet until half past nine the next morning, none of us moving quickly after our late-night tiny heart attacks and the wine we glugged to get back to sleep.

Dawk flew out the door after chugging a way-too-hot cup of coffee so he could open the store at ten. Me? I took my time with my coffee, enjoying the bitter taste with hints of walnuts.

Lynnae poured a bit of coconut milk in her coffee and joined me at the table. "You look like you haven't slept in a month," she told me.

"Oh, thanks, bestie. I appreciate your kind words. Especially considering you look perfect, as always." Her raven twists were shiny, her skin was bright, and she wore a bright-pink cropped cardigan with high-waisted, wide-legged black pants.

My hair was sticking up in eight places and I wore a huge, holey T-shirt that said "Vampires do it in the dark."

"Aww, and I appreciate *your* kind words," she echoed.

Her face grew serious. "Look, I know Dawk wants you to solve this ASAP, but you aren't any use as an investigator or a business owner if you burn yourself out. Your body needs rest. You've been doing too much."

"Ughhhhh," I said. "You're right. I know you are." My body knew too. Little needles had inserted themselves in all my joints, all over my back, and inside my neck. Every movement knocked against the needles.

Matilda flew through her doggy door, full of energy after her morning backyard exploration time. She lapped up some water before barreling straight at Lynnae.

"Oh no!" my roommate told her. "Get those muddy paws away from me."

Laughing, I leaned over to corral my goofy pup.

Standing up and backing away from the table, my roomie downed her coffee and set the mug on the granite countertop. "That's my signal to go to work."

"Tell Calder I'll see him promptly at 5:00 p.m. to start baking." I narrowed my eyes jokingly. "You too. No getting caught up in your research."

"Yes, yes. We'll all be there."

It was Monday, the day before Valentine's Day. The time had come to start baking a million dog cakes. I'd scheduled myself the day off, knowing I would need to rest if I was going to help in the bakery all night.

You might be thinking, *Josie, why didn't Isa just bake the cakes over the past few days instead of all at once?* One word: freshness. The cakes might be canine in nature, but they needed to be soft with crisp icing. If the cakes were dry and cracked, we were likely to have a host of upset customers tomorrow.

I tried to pull myself together, but I couldn't do it. My body needed rest, so I crawled back into bed and pulled my four blankets over me. My little Scottie pushed into my armpit, her head on my shoulder. Despite the coffee, I dropped right into sleep.

Every ninety minutes or so, I'd shoot awake, covered in sweat, images dancing through my mind of Maggie with a stake in her arm or Eddie chasing me down Vein Street, his mother running behind him with a rolling pin.

Exhaustion would pull me back under each time until my alarm went off at half past two.

Matilda stretched, her butt in the air, and let out a little grumble.

"Aww, big stretchies!" I said in my cutesy voice reserved only for animals.

I did a few big stretchies too before dragging myself into the shower, where I blasted an audiobook about a woman locked in a library with a murderer.

I skipped makeup, other than a quick swipe of mascara, figuring it would melt off in the blazing bakery kitchen. Dark jeans, black sneakers, and a lightweight purple top on, I finally looked like a person.

I had some time before I needed to leave. Feeling completely stuck on the case, I had no desire to spin my wheels about the attacks. My brain still craved something to focus on, though, so I slumped on the couch with the entry/exit logs I'd extorted.

The names started to blur together after twenty minutes. Maybe I was too tired for the task. But then, just after my bobbing head jerked back up, one of the names caught my eye.

Hollow, Belinda 10/08/22 21:17

Just after 9:00 p.m. the night before the first note was left, Belinda Hollow entered Arteria Falls. The name looked familiar, but I didn't think I knew anyone named Belinda.

Wide awake now, I grabbed the files corresponding to the second note. Using my finger to track the names, I flicked my eyes down the pages.

There it was. Belinda Hollow had entered Arteria Falls at half past ten the night before I received the second note.

I grabbed the files from my grandfather's disappearance. I had a whole week's worth, but now that I was looking for a specific name, it wouldn't take long to search.

Flipping through the first four days leading up to the disappearance slowly drained my hope, but on day five, I stood up, arms in the air, and yelled, "I'VE GOT YOU, BELINDA HOLLOW!"

Matilda sat up and let out a few happy yips, feeding off my energy.

"That's right, girl. We've got her. Except," I sat down and looked at my little dog, "who in the heck is Belinda Hollow?"

A quick internet search failed me. I ran out of time before I could research further, so I hid all the files in my room and clipped Matilda's leash to her collar.

After dropping Matilda off with my mother, who delayed me fifteen minutes with gossip about who the attacker might be—none of which made any sense, especially Roxie's theory about a local dog breeder trying to entice people into buying dogs for security purposes—I rolled into the boutique.

"Hey, boss," Dawk said from the dog-treat aisle. "Your nose looks frozen."

"I think it's about to fall off my face. Nineteen degrees! It's way too cold."

He grabbed three more bags of locally made peanut-butter dog treats and placed them on the shelf in front of him. "I heard it's supposed to get down to ten degrees tomorrow and five degrees on Wednesday when the storm hits."

"Great, can't wait for the ridiculously cold snowstorm. Was it busy today?" I rolled back to my office, my chest still filled with excitement over finding Belinda. Dawk walked right behind carrying the empty treat box.

"Not really. We sold a bunch more Valentine's toys and treats as well as a decent amount of food, but that's it."

"People are probably hiding from the cold. They'll have to brave it tomorrow to come pick up their dog cakes, though."

Dawk broke down the box. "I'm so looking forward to that frenzy. Hey, I'm going to ring myself up for a giant marrow bone. Silver finished her last one already."

"C'mon, you can tell me. The bone is for you, isn't it? An after-blood snack?"

He laughed. "Right. You caught me."

"Seriously, though, Silver's commitment to destruction will never cease to amaze me."

Silver was Dawk's mom's dog. She had a silky—you guessed it—silver coat and the sweetest disposition, but she was a destroyer. Dawk had been buying her marrow bones for months now to help keep her busy.

The shop was still open for another hour when 5:00 p.m. arrived, so after finishing off the next week's schedule—my most hated task—I left Dawk to his stocking and wheeled next door.

Isa's Eats was already closed, so I banged on the door until Hadley let me inside. "Oh my stars, it's so cold out there."

"I'm practically an icicle after just sixty seconds outside."

She gestured for me to follow her. "Come to the back. The ovens are flaming."

Isa was surprisingly calm. I'd expected her to be a ball of nerves, curls bursting from her ponytail, voice shaky with nerves. But she gave me a quick hug, took my coat, and with unexpected composure, showed me the binder with all her plans for the night.

Hadley, who'd been organizing oat flour, ended up just unlocking the door after the third time someone banged on it.

By fifteen after five, Disha, Lynnae, Calder, and Elm had joined us. We all gathered around the huge metal table that took up half the kitchen.

I longed to pull Lynnae aside to tell her about Belinda, but it would have to wait. Someone would overhear.

"Where's Dawk?" Disha asked, hands on hips.

"At soccer practice. He goes right after the shop closes on Mondays." I spoke up as she started to complain. "He's been really on edge lately, given the attacks, so I didn't want him to cancel on practice. When practice is over, he'll join us."

Disha dropped her hands. "Okay, I guess he gets a pass." She looked at Lynnae and Calder. "Hey, what's the healing time for a vamp getting bitten? And do the bites leave scars? And what about—"

Isa cleared her throat. Disha, a human who was still pretty new to the vampire world and loved asking questions about vamps, gave her a sheepish grin. "Sorry."

The baker smiled back, a little spark passing between the two women. "Thank you all for coming," she said to the room. "The sooner we get started, the sooner we can finish."

With that, Isa launched into how many cakes could fit in the oven at once, her calculations about time to prep each batch, and how many stations we needed to most efficiently bust out cakes.

"I've got positions for you all, but we can switch around so no one gets too bored. Disha, you'll measure peanut butter. Elm, you'll measure the other wet ingredients. Hadley, you'll take the first stand mixer. Lynnae, you'll add dry ingredients after the wet is mixed. I'll run the second mixer. Calder, you'll pour into the cake molds. Josie, you'll take the cakes in and out of the oven.

"We're going to focus on the baking first, then once we're far enough along, we'll move to icing. We've got the laptop that's connected to the icing printer pre-loaded with everyone's orders, so it should be quick once we're ready to print on the icing sheets. I've got extra edible ink cartridges too. Elm, I think you'll run the printer when it's time as you're the most tech savvy."

They gave a little bow. "I'd be honored, Isa."

We all laughed and moved to our first stations.

Chapter Nineteen

By half past seven, we'd found a smooth groove. The team was working together almost flawlessly, just a few spills here and there.

"We'll rotate positions in thirty minutes, everyone," Isa yelled. She didn't need to yell, as the kitchen wasn't that big, but her enthusiasm was keeping our spirits up.

Except mine, because I had the easiest—and most boring—job. When a full batch of cakes was ready, I slid them into one of the ovens. At the ding of the timer thirty minutes later, I pulled the cakes out and slid them into the oven racks.

I was in between batches, spinning Isa's office chair in circles. I'd gotten sick of my wheelchair and pulled her chair over to the ovens instead.

Calder was the closest to me. His job was not only to pour batter but to make sure more pans were ready to go. When a batch of cakes was cool enough, he'd flip them over and pull the pans.

Currently oiling the next set of pans, he asked, "What's on your mind, Jos?"

"The case. All the details."

Disha called out over the whirring of the mixers, "At least you'll both be safe in here with all of us! Well, once Dawk gets here."

"True," I conceded. "But what about tomorrow night? And everyone else who got hearts?"

"How many days since the last attack?" Elm asked.

"Four. The first two attacks were a few days apart, so it's time." It might've actually been past time, if the attacker was outside our house last night, trying to get to me or Dawk. Would they try someone else tonight?

Lynnae dumped some flour into the bowl in front of her. "Maybe we can help you. Tell us everything."

So I did. "The most frustrating parts to me are why the victims were chosen and why the items were left at the scene. I don't understand the little trinkets the attacker left behind at all. They left three things behind at each scene—the stake, a heart, and an object. But *different* objects. Why are they different? And what do they mean?"

"What were they again?" Isa asked.

"A scale for Maggie and a shield for Niall."

"You said Maggie has no idea why the scale was left, so let's consider it more broadly. What do scales usually mean?" she asked.

The timer went off, and I stood up, using a collapsible cane I'd brought with me. "Justice. I keep going back to justice. But how could staking and biting Maggie bring justice?"

"You're still thinking about Maggie. Maybe it's not about her. Maybe it represents justice in general. Justice against all blonds or something," Calder mused.

Elm poured coconut milk in a huge measuring cup. "Maybe it's not justice at all. The scale could represent something else, maybe balance? The two sides of the scale in balance."

Hmm. That was a good idea. "That's genius," I told them as I slipped the last cake onto the racks. "What kind of balance could it be? Balancing your life, the balance between nature and—"

Disha cut me off. "Balancing the books. Like in accounting."

I spun around, my eyes wide.

"Sorry, Jos. I didn't mean to cut you off. My accountant called me earlier, so it was on my mind."

"You. Are. A. Genius," I said, punctuating each word with a bang on the metal table.

Elm caught on quickly. "Niall is an accountant."

"Exactly!" I exclaimed. "The trinket next to Maggie wasn't about her, it was about *the next victim*."

"Dracula's cape," Calder said. "We might be able to figure out the attacker's next target."

I sat back down and tapped my foot. "A shield. A shield. A shield. A—"

"Yes, we know it's a shield," Lynnae said. "Tell us what it looked like. Are we talking Captain America?"

"I have no idea! Niall told me it looked like it came off a ceramic figurine." I pulled my phone out of my back pocket. "Let me text him."

Ten minutes later, my phone buzzed. "Holy fangs. He has a picture of it. After the attack, the police had him send it to his wife to see if she knew anything about it." I looked up at everyone, more excited than I'd been in days. "I can do a reverse image search!"

Isa came over to look at the search results. "Achilles' shield? What the heck?"

"Maybe it's someone into Greek mythology," Hadley suggested, scraping the sides of the bowl as her mixer spun. "Or maybe it has something to do with Achilles specifically."

"Let's think," Isa said. "Achilles was a key player in the Trojan War. He was a hero and a great warrior. Brad Pitt played him in a movie. His only vulnerability was his heel."

I smiled up at her. "Wow, you know a lot about Achilles."

She shrugged. "I watch documentaries at night."

It was time to put another batch in the oven, so I slid the cakes in, considering everything Isa had said. The Trojan War was well known. Could this be about the Trojan Horse? Something that looks legitimate but turns out to be harmful?

Achilles' heel was referenced just as often if not more. Could the shield represent a weakness? Or what about the more literal meaning, the tendon that runs from the calf to the heel?

Wait. My cousin's words flashed through my brain. *Maybe he can help me with a bit of Achilles tendinitis.*

The cake I was holding slipped through my fingers and crashed to the floor.

Calder ran over. "Jos! Are you okay?"

My hands were still out in front of me, where I'd held the cake. "Achilles tendinitis. Achilles tendinitis!"

I grabbed my cane and started heading out of the kitchen in search of Zippy.

Lynnae cut me off at the door. "What, Josie? What is it?"

"Dawk has Achilles tendinitis."

Everyone stopped moving and grew silent.

"Fangs," Calder said after a minute. "But he'll be safe now, right? The attacks have been in the middle of the night. It's only eight."

"We don't know that for sure! Maybe that was the most convenient time to attack Maggie and Niall.

Maybe by Dawk staying with us, we've forced the attacker to change things up."

"That's a good point," Disha said. "Dawk probably shouldn't be alone."

"You mean like right now, as his soccer practice is finishing up?"

I tried to push past Lynnae again, but Elm joined her. "Let me through!" I shouted.

"Josie," Calder said gently, coming to stand next to me. "It's not safe for you to go alone. Let me go with you. Please?"

"And me," Elm said decisively.

"Get your coats."

Chapter Twenty

"He's not answering his phone."

Calder, who had insisted on driving, flipped on the van's turn signal. "How are we going to find him?"

"I rode with him one night so I could meet up with you and Lynnae at the lab. A lot of the guys park in the garage next to the rec center, but he's too cheap, so he always parks on Magnolia."

"What part of Magnolia?" Elm asked.

"Under the big trees."

Calder clutched the steering wheel so hard his knuckles turned white. "That part of campus is empty at night."

We rode in silence as Calder drove us way too fast across Arteria Falls.

Squeezing the seat as hard as I could, I tried to keep my cool. Just because Dawk would be alone in the dark after practice didn't mean the attacker would go after him.

Unable to wait any longer, I pulled out my phone. "Let me call him again."

No answer.

As we turned onto Magnolia, I saw why. My phone fell to the floor. "Fangs! Fangs! Fangs!"

A fireplace poker swung through the air toward my cousin, who deflected the hit with something thick and white. Was that…a jumbo marrow bone?

A dark figure drew the poker back again, this time aimed at Dawk's stomach. Calder hit the horn as we sped toward the fight.

The black-clad, ski-masked person attached to the poker startled and froze for a second before fleeing between two dark buildings.

"DAWK!" I screamed as we pulled up next to him. Out of the car in a flash, not even grabbing my cane, I grabbed onto my cousin and squeezed him. Sweat dripped off him, and he smelled like gym socks, but I didn't care.

Dawk was like a brother to me. We were attached at the hip as kids, always playing, always laughing. And—in case you hadn't noticed, given that we work together and still hang out—we were still pretty darn attached.

"Josie! Can you ease up a bit? I'm trying to breathe here."

"Sorry." I let go and moved back a few inches, looking him up and down. Other than a scratch on his neck, he looked fine.

"Are you okay?" Calder asked Dawk as he handed me my cane and phone.

Dawk's passenger door was open, his gym bag on the seat. He pushed it to the floor and climbed into the car, still holding the plastic-wrapped bone.

"Holy fangs. My heart is pounding like crazy," he said.

Calder went into doctor mode. "Take a few deep breaths. Yep, just like that." He stepped forward. "Can I look at your neck?"

Dawk turned his neck, and I noticed his fangs were out.

Ever so gently, Calder turned my cousin's neck a little more to catch the light. "It's just a surface wound, but it needs to be cleaned and bandaged."

I turned to ask Elm to call the cops, but they were nowhere to be found. "Where's Elm?"

"They took off after the attacker," Calder told me.

I called the cops instead, and a few minutes after I hung up, Elm came jogging back, their rapid breaths foggy in the cold air. "Holy stars, they're fast. I lost them back by the library."

I walked to the van, which was parked in the middle of the road, and pulled my notebook out of my backpack.

Big, wet snowflakes started to fall around us as I limped back. The snow coming through the tall ash trees would have been gorgeous any other night.

Thank goodness my notebook was designed to get wet.

I jumped right into investigator mode. "Did you notice anything about them that could help?" I'd only seen the attacker for a few seconds, so I was hoping Elm had seen something.

They bent over, hands on their knees. "Umm, they had a black cross-body satchel."

I huffed. It was probably filled with all their little attack goodies. You know—the heart, the stake, and whatever trinket they had planned to leave next to a bleeding, unconscious Dawk.

"Anything else?" I asked.

"Broad shoulders, and they were shorter than me, I think, but not short."

Dawk spoke up, "Yeah, definitely shorter than you, but still tall."

"Oh!" Elm reached into their back pocket. "This flew out of the satchel."

I held my hand out. A heart. A *construction paper* heart.

"What happened, Dawk?" I needed to get his story before he forgot anything. And before the police showed up and got in the way.

"I was putting my duffel on the seat." He patted the bag. "With the attacks happening in the middle of the night, I wasn't being *super* cautious, but I was more aware of my surroundings than normal. So when I heard a slight scuffle on the asphalt, I whipped around."

He pulled in a deep breath before continuing. "All I saw at first was something coming at my head, so I pulled back, and it hit me in the neck. I kinda fell backward into the seat. I was groping around for anything that could help when I found the bone I'd bought for Silver. The attacker lifted the bar—I think it was a fire poker, but it all happened so fast—and I held up the bone to take the blow. I managed to stand back up and push them away, but they just came back at me. Then you guys showed up."

"Dirty Dracula," I mumbled, rubbing my hands up and down my arms. As the adrenaline wore off, the cold was setting in—and the pain too.

Calder, a living saint, noticed and opened the SUV's back door. I squeezed his arm, his jacket wet from the snow, and mouthed my thanks.

Dawk looked around the headrest at me. "How did you know to come?"

I explained about the trinkets and the connection to his Achilles tendinitis. "Once I realized you were the target, I just…had a bad feeling. That noise Matilda heard last night? I was worried it was the attacker and that they'd try to get at you another time, another way."

"Thank the stars we got here in time," Calder said. "With the way they were trying to hit you, you could have been killed, not just knocked out."

My cousin put his head in his hands, fluffing his hair with his fingers.

"How could they possibly know about my Achilles tendinitis? I've only talked about it with my soccer buds and you."

I tapped my chin thoughtfully. "We were alone, but someone could have overheard you and your pals at soccer practice."

Elm chimed in, "Lots of people use the indoor track around the field this time of year. Maybe the attacker is a runner. I mean, that would explain how they overheard and how they got away from me so easily."

Dawk leaned on the seat. "I guess someone could have been listening to me talk about my tendon."

A spark lit in my mind. "Someone was spying on you during your practice on campus. And someone watches Maggie on campus."

"Just a coincidence? Or something more?" Calder wondered, voicing my thoughts.

We heard sirens coming our way. I reached through the seat to grip Dawk's shoulder. "Before the cops get here and distract us all, do you want me to call Everly or your mom?" I gave him a devilish grin. "Or my mom? Yep, I'm calling my mom."

He groaned. "Fangs. I think I'd rather have the attacker back."

Isa's ponytail was like the Grinch's heart—it had grown three sizes by the time we pulled the last Cupid cake from the oven. Her poor curls were frazzled, she was covered in batter, and she looked like she was about to fall asleep standing.

"What time did you wake up today, or I guess yesterday, Isa?" I asked.

"Four in the morning."

Lynnae whistled. "It's 2:00 a.m. now. You need to go take care of yourself."

She waved off our concerns. "I have to start the normal baking by half past four. If I sleep now, I'll be so much groggier."

Disha came up and untied Isa's apron. "C'mon. Even if you don't sleep, you need to get out of the bakery. Let's go to my house for a couple hours."

Isa nodded, her eyes distant.

All the dishes were done. All the surfaces were shiny again. At least Isa would have a clean start to the day.

"I'll get a few hours of sleep and come in early to help you, Isa," Hadley said as she shut off the bakery lights.

After Dawk had been dragged away by both our mothers, whispering a small "help me" that only I'd been able to hear, the rest of us had returned to the bakery.

We'd been gone for a couple hours, each having given a statement to the responding officers, so the baking had been quite delayed. Calder, Elm, and I had jumped back in, but we'd still been pretty stressed. Who would have thought that seeing an attempt to bash your friend on the head with a fire poker would leave you quite rattled?

The more I'd calmed, the more my body had hurt. Calder had eventually asked Isa to put me in charge of the laptop and icing printer so I'd have to stay seated.

"Josie," he'd said as he'd leaned over me, his breath warm in my ear, "just take it easy. I'd suggest you go home, but then you'd be alone." A worried expression had crossed his face. "We don't know what this maniac will do next. They might have gone after Dawk, but you fit the victim profile too. So stay here, but just relax."

Relaxation hadn't been in the cards. In between printing multicolored icing sheets that said "Happy Valentine's Day, Riley," or "You're the Only One for Me,

Mildred," or "Who's my Cutie Patootie?," I'd agonized over the investigation.

I was still agonizing as we all pulled on our coats to finally go home.

Dawk was attacked at the college. He'd likely been overheard at the college. Maggie had a creepy watcher at the college.

And what about Niall? He didn't work there. I hadn't had a reason to ask if he ever spent time on campus. Two in the morning was a bit late to text, so I'd have to contact him later.

And who would be next? Would they be connected to the college too?

And why the college? Did something happen to the attacker there, causing them to design this whole scheme as some kind of revenge?

"Joooosiiieeee," Elm sing-songed.

"Huh? What?"

Everyone was waiting by the door, staring at me.

"Did you hear us?" Lynnae asked. "Calder's driving the van and staying the night."

I was about to protest, but I was too tired and...I wanted him there. Knowing he was nearby would ease my worries, make me feel safe. I knew it would make him feel better too.

So I shut my trap and got in the van.

"Frickity frick, it's beyond freezing in here! We aren't undead enough for these temperatures." At least it had stopped snowing. Only a light layer dusted the ground.

Calder laughed and turned on the seat warmers. "Let's hope that helps." He pulled away from the curb and started down Vein Street. "If you don't mind, I'll be driving us at snail speeds to make up for the turbo speeds earlier."

"But you're such an excellent fast driver! The way you dodged that Dodge when we careened onto Arteria Avenue was *impressive*."

"I have years and years of Mario Kart to thank for those mad skills."

I clapped my hands but the sound was muted by my eight layers of gloves. "Oh, I haven't played Mario Kart in so long!"

"We can play tomorrow night if you want. Or I guess tonight."

Right. Our not-a-date Valentine's Day hang at his house. The leftover coconut flour brownies I'd stolen from Isa's pastry case swirled in my stomach.

I had avoided thinking about it. I was nervous, but I could handle that. No, I'd been avoiding it because there was a huge part of me screaming to just let it be a real date. The only way to shut that part up was to act like the not-date wasn't happening.

You're probably thinking, *Josie, you dingbat! Let that part out! Embrace your desire to be with Calder. He's amazing. Don't let him get away.*

And you would be right. He is amazing. So, taking a deep breath, I didn't make any jokes or try to deflect. I caught his eye when we stopped at the next light. "Calder, that would be amazing. I can't wait."

Lips pulling into a little smile, he said, "Me too."

His smile lasted all the way home and into the next morning. Mine too.

Chapter Twenty-One

G littery snow amplified the light in the living room the next morning, blinding me for a second when I opened my bedroom door.

Calder was asleep on the piles of sleeping bags and camping pads Dawk had been using as a bed. All four blankets I'd given him were pushed to the side. One arm was over his head, the other rested on his stomach where a small piece of skin was exposed above his boxers.

That's right—his boxers. Lynnae and I didn't have any Calder-sized pajama pants, so he'd had to make do without.

Which was all well and good when the blankets were on top of him.

After yesterday, I desperately needed Zippy instead of my crutch, which was perfect—Zippy was nearly silent on our wood floors.

Relocating my gaze to his face and only his face, I undid the brakes, rolling ever so slowly toward Calder. When I got close, I leaned forward, reached down, and booped his nose.

His eyes shot open, and he sat straight up. The confused look on his face was so adorable that I just wanted to pinch his cheeks.

When he looked down and noted the state of his blankets, he froze.

"Calder, I've seen boxers before. Now, put on some pants or don't—makes no difference to me—and let's make coffee."

He opted for the pants.

"What's on your schedule today?" I asked. "Hopefully nothing too early, because it's already nine."

Running a hand through his wavy tresses, which somehow still looked perfect, he said, "Naw. No meetings or anything this morning." His face lit up, his dimple appearing as he continued, "I've got the whole morning to work on my comparison of human and vampire gastroenterological processing of sugars, especially—"

And off he went into the details of something super scientific. Between Calder and Lynnae, I had a lot of experience pretending to understand such details, so I nodded and made interested sounds in all the appropriate spots.

"Anyway, I'm sure I'm boring the fangs out of you."

"No," I told him, reaching out to grasp his forearm. "You're not boring me at all." While I had no idea what he was talking about, I loved how excited it made him.

He clasped my forearm too, so we looked like we were in the middle of a secret handshake when my roommate appeared.

Lynnae raised an eyebrow as we snatched our arms back, but didn't harass us about it. She grabbed a mug instead. "Coffee. Tell me there's coffee left."

"Duh. I would never neglect your coffee needs after you spent all night helping me and Isa make dog cakes."

"That's what I like to hear. So did you sleep or just think about the Heart Attacks all night?"

The Heart Attacks...why hadn't I been calling them that this whole time? I took a sip of the bitter dark roast I'd chosen. "My body didn't give me a choice. I went right to sleep. Did you guys sleep?"

They both bobbed their heads.

"Are you going to the shop today or investigating?" Calder asked.

"Both. Dawk already texted that he's still coming to work today. Knowing him, he needs the distraction right now. I'm relieved, as we've got a zillion dog cakes to distribute. Lacey is coming in too, so I'm hoping to have at least a bit of time to focus on the Heart

Attacks." I paused to refill my cup. "This connection to the college means something. I'm sure of it. Something else is ticking away in my brain, but I can't quite reach it yet." I held my hand out and made a fist.

Calder set his cup down. "It will come to you soon, Jos."

Lynnae set her cup down too. "C'mon, boss. Let's go to work." She ushered Calder out the front door, leaving me alone with my thoughts. It was the perfect moment for a Matilda hug, to let her little body warm me, but she was still with my mom. Sighing, I threw on some clothes and rushed to the shop.

"At least the cakes are paid for, so it should be quick to hand them out. I'm hoping the owners might buy some extra goodies, though. We'll see."

My keys rattled, my cold hands unsteady as I unlocked the door. Dawk leaned around me and pushed the access button.

"Go on, Matilda!" The little dog wagged her tail as she ran past me into the shop, eager to get out of the cold.

"I hope it's easy. I didn't get any sleep. After I was taken *against my will* to your mom's house, both of our moms sat up all night talking outside the guest room door. Your mom had a baseball bat, and I could hear her slapping it against her palm. Over and over and over."

I laughed. "That sounds like my mom. She brought a baseball bat to my house that night I was attacked a few months back."

"It's her weapon of choice, I guess. Even Matilda slept restlessly. She kept trying to crawl on my head."

Matilda turned around at the sound of her name, her fluffy eyebrows raised.

"Good girl, Matilda! Sleep right on his face next time."

"Har-har-har," Dawk said. "Very funny."

I stopped rolling at Reggie's kennel. "Do you want to feed him or should I?"

"I'll do it."

Smiling up at my cousin, I told him, "Good. You can take him to my office to feed him and give him time to stretch his legs. It'll be good for both of you."

When I'd parked behind Dawk and Matilda on Vein Street, I'd gotten a look at my cousin before he could put on his macho face. His eyes had darted up and down the brick sidewalk, his fear obvious. When his eyes had landed on me, he'd given me a tired smile, the fear receding behind an unruffled mask.

He'd be quite ruffled until the attacker was caught.

With a long, drawn-out sigh that was more like a groan, I got the store ready for the day. Behind the sales counter, along the back wall of the shop, Dawk had set up three folding tables the day before. I pulled out a few white tablecloths and more than a few bags of heart confetti and BE MINE stickers.

Some things are just too difficult while I'm in the wheelchair. By the third time I'd rammed my leg into a table leg while trying to straighten a tablecloth, I pulled out my cane and stood up.

That's when I saw it. Right as I pulled the last corner into place, I noticed a little ceramic bird figurine sitting on top of a bookcase full of pet care and training books. Next to it, a chess piece lay on its side.

The knight. Protector, defender. The only chess piece besides the pawn that can kick off the game.

It'd been out of my view while I was sitting, but I could see it clearly now. How did the attacker get in? And when? Security cameras for the shop had just moved up my priority list. At least it would be a business expense.

I tapped over to the bookcase, picked up the heavy chess piece, and slipped it into my pocket

A grayish-brown bird? No clue what that meant. Bird symbology is endless. But the knight? That was for me. A little message from the attacker. I'd protected my cousin. Successfully defended him. And I'd kicked off a modified game. They knew I was onto them.

I was tempted to pick up the bird too, but instead, I took out my phone. After snapping a few photos, I called the non-emergency police number and left a message for the detective in charge of the case.

Would they believe that the trinkets were linked to the next victim? Would they try to find the next target before the attacker struck again? I couldn't count on it.

Just as Dawk came back out front, Reggie in his arms, the front door shot open and a bouncy blur shot through the store.

"Ohmyfangsyou'reherewehavesomuchtodo."

The trinket forgotten, I tapped over to the vibrating human standing next to the tables.

"Isa! What is going on? You look like you've had a gallon of coffee?"

"Just one gallon?" Dawk muttered.

She jumped from foot to foot. "Yep, yep, yep. So much coffee. So much cake."

"Right." I held my hand out in front of me. "Operation Transport Cupid Cakes, begin!"

You might be thinking, *Josie, why not just have the customers pick the cakes up from Isa's directly?*

Here's why. Isa's bakery closes early. We expected that most cakes would be picked up between 4:00 and 6:00 p.m. when folks were done working. I also hoped that I could sell a lot of dog merch to the cake-picker-uppers. Isa was getting most of the cake money with the expectation that I'd make a lot in add-on sales. I couldn't do that if they didn't come into the store.

Moving the cakes would be too difficult for me, and I needed to be in the store in case a customer came in. So while Dawk followed Isa back to the bakery, I dumped the confetti on the tables and slapped the heart stickers on the tablecloth overhang. I also grabbed my pain kit from a drawer under the counter and slapped on as much Bengay as I could before the first cakes arrived.

Boxes and boxes of white cakes came into the boutique on a two-tiered cart Isa owned. Over the past few days, Hadley and Isa had been prepping empty boxes for the cakes, stapling a ticket for each order onto the thin cardboard. After we had finished icing the last few cakes, all we'd had to do was slip them into the boxes.

Back in my chair, I helped organize them alphabetically and—voilà—we were ready.

Isa stood to the side, looking like she was about to cry. "We did it. It's over."

"Over for you," Dawk whispered. I shook my head at him before rolling over to Isa.

"C'mon, love. Let's get you back to your store. Hadley said she has things under control with the customers. Tuesdays aren't that busy, right?"

She nodded. "Pretty slow."

"Okay, well why don't you go take a little nap in your office until Hadley needs you?"

"A nap?" she said, almost as if she didn't understand me. "A nap. Okay, a nap." She'd gone from zoom to zombie quickly, all the energy draining from her.

Lacey came in at eleven, but we'd been slow so far—just two cake pick-ups and two customers replenishing their canned cat food.

"Josie," my cousin said not long after Lacey clocked in. "I think we can handle this. Like you predicted, the cakes aren't moving fast at this time of day. Maybe you should…" he trailed off.

"Go investigate? I've been thinking that too. I'll go, but call me the second you get busy, okay? You're too tired, and I don't want you to be overwhelmed." I pivoted my chair to Lacey, who was setting her jacket under the counter. "Lacey!"

"Erm, yes?"

"Do not let Dawk out of your sight."

Lacey looked between me and my cousin, her face blank. "Umm, okay?" She didn't know what had happened last night yet, but I was sure Dawk would fill her in.

I gave them one last instruction. "If the cops show up, call me." I hadn't told Dawk about the bird trinket. He had enough on his plate, but he'd find out if the cops came. It was also possible they'd come by with more questions or information for Dawk, and I wanted to know absolutely anything they said.

"Cops?" Lacey asked.

"Dawk…are you okay telling Lacey or do you want me to—"

He waved me off. "It's fine. I'll tell her. Leave, please!"

Before I left, puffy coat zipped all the way up for the fifteen degrees that awaited me outside, I remembered one last thing. Making exaggerated kissy-faces at them as I wheeled backward to the door, I said, "Happy Valentine's Day to my lovely Matilda's VamPets employees!"

Chapter Twenty-Two

Despite the chill making my bones rattle, I left my van where it was. My first stop was just down Vein Street.

My thickest fleece gloves weren't enough to stop the first trail of numbness up my fingers, so I was relieved when I arrived at a little shop with a blue awning and a colorful display in the window.

Jackie, owner of Jackie's Crafts, was on a step ladder, trying to reach a high shelf, when I opened the door, which was thankfully light. The threshold was higher than normal, though. I struggled to get over it, gripping the door to help pull me through. The little bell over the door jingled and jingled until I finally pulled myself inside.

Frozen on the stepladder, Jackie's mouth hung open a bit before she snapped out of it and jumped down, surprisingly spry for her age. "Oh my stars! I never realized how difficult that hump would be for wheelchair users."

"It's okay. It happens. How about you make it up to me by answering a few questions?" I said, my tone jesting.

With a laugh, she maneuvered through the tight aisles of her shop until she was standing next to the high sales counter. "Crafting questions?"

"Sort of." I slipped my backpack off the handles of my chair and dug inside. "Do you recognize these?" I asked, holding up the hearts.

"Oh dear." Jackie stepped closer and took the hearts in her small hands. "Are these *the* hearts everyone is talking about?"

I nodded. "Do you sell hearts like this? That are already cut, I mean?"

"No." She set the construction paper down and rubbed the other heart with her fingers. "I recognize this paper, though."

Bingo. That's exactly what I'd hoped for.

She turned to the back of the store, signaling me to follow.

The store was short on space, so the built-in shelves on all four walls went all the way to the ceiling. Half of the back wall was stocked with paper in every color and price point you could imagine. Jackie went straight to a shelf at her eye level.

"Here it is," she said, sliding the fancy red paper out of its cubbyhole.

The small pack of paper carried quite the price tag. "You're sure this is it?"

"Yep. Positive."

"Do you by chance remember selling any recently?"

Jackie shook her head. "No, I'm sorry. I sell so much paper."

"Makes sense. A paper like this wouldn't be bought by just anyone, right?"

"It's usually for serious crafters."

"And the other two hearts are just plain construction paper," I said, thinking aloud.

"It's really strange that whoever made these hearts used such different papers. I wouldn't expect someone who owns this level of paper," she tapped the pack in her hand, "to use construction paper too. I noticed the glue was different as well."

"It's as if two different people made the hearts."

I banged on the door, fluffy flamingos bouncing around on their wreath. I'd already hit the doorbell about twenty times too. "Judith! Open up!"

"Ouch!" I'd been using so much force that my ulna slipped out of place. That had happened to me many times in recent years, so I just popped it back into place. Picking up my cane, I was about to resume banging on the door with it, but the door flew open.

Judith was wearing a fuzzy pink robe with—you guessed it—a flamingo on the left breast. A pink towel was wrapped around her hair.

"What in the fangs is going on, Josie? Are you here for Eddie again?"

"No," I said. "I'm here for *you*."

Her face paled. "Well, as you can see, I'm not ready for guests."

She moved to close the door, so just like on my last visit, I stuck my combat boot out to block it.

"You know, that's quite rude," she said, her eyebrows pinched.

"Is it now? And it's not rude to leave hearts for all the blond vamps around town, scaring them half to undeath?"

I was upset, but not enough to miss out on a vampire pun opportunity.

With a grumble, Judith let go of the door and shuffled inside, her pink slippers dragging across the immaculate floors. I followed her into flamingo hell.

She perched on the edge of a beige Chesterfield sofa, not because she was nervous, but because the back 80 percent of the seat cushion was covered with flamingo throw pillows and one full-sized stuffed flamingo.

Not the taxidermied kind of stuffed, but the toy kind. If it was the former, I'd have hobbled out of the house screaming.

"How'd you know?" Judith asked once I was seated on the most flamingo-free surface I could find.

"The two paper types confused me. My cousin got a construction paper heart, I got a fancy heart, and a construction paper heart was left on the door to my pet boutique. I thought maybe the attacker ran out of construction paper."

I pulled the hearts out of my backpack. "I thought maybe Eddie had access to construction paper through his activities at work, but ran out of it and bought something different."

Judith's head dropped into her hands. "Please. He's a good boy." She looked back up, tears streaming down her face. "He just gets angry and doesn't know how to handle it. I just wanted to protect him."

Weeping now, she leaned down to her knees, her hair towel slipping to the floor. "I…was…trying to…get…him…help."

"Judith! Eddie is NOT the attacker," I said, my voice firm.

She sat up, her wet hair standing in all directions like a plume of feathers. "What?"

"I saw the attacker last night. They went after my cousin, but he fought back. My friends and I got there while they were fighting. The attacker had a ski mask on, but they were way too tall to be Eddie."

Relief rippled through Judith's body, from her face to her shoulders to her toes, everything relaxed. "Thank the Goddess!" she cried out, tears dripping down her chin. "I was so sure it was him."

"So you left the hearts around town to throw the police off?" I held up the fancy heart. "I'm assuming you had this expensive paper in your craft room already."

"Yes. As soon as I heard about the second attack, I started cutting hearts. The fancy paper was all I had, but I was too worried to care about the price. I thought if I left enough hearts, the police wouldn't know where to focus their investigation."

"You were right. Judith, do you realize that throwing these fake hearts in the mix could have led to someone being seriously injured? My cousin was *attacked* last night."

"But no one was dying!" she insisted. "They were just getting a bit hurt."

I snorted. "Really? Being knocked out, bitten, and staked is 'just a bit hurt'? If you hadn't thrown everything off, the police could have focused on the actual hearts. They would have known who the next victims were!"

"But I was getting Eddie help! His father was flying in, and we were going to take him to a facility down in Fangstaff—"

"You were going to WHAT?" a shocked voice asked. Eddie came around the corner from the kitchen a moment later wearing a thick coat with a dusting of snow on it. He must have come in a back door.

Judith jumped up. "No, no. It's okay. Josie explained it to me. You're too short to be the attacker."

"Oh, that's why you believe I'm not behind the attacks? Because I'm too short? What in the actual fangs, Ma?"

"There were so many signs! You're always so angry. Always talking about how people would be sorry they'd crossed you." She put a hand on his shoulder. "The bugs are a bit creepy too. Especially how you save the dead ones. And you told me some blond girl had rejected you. I thought it was the first victim. And the attacker was biting them!"

"It's not like I throw dead bugs in a shoebox. I use display cases, like in museums." He shrugged off her hand. "Lots of girls reject me, so what? Their loss. I don't go around biting them." He ran a hand down his face. "It's all talk, Ma. I wouldn't actually hurt anyone. Why would you think I'd bite someone?"

Her face flushed. "I know that's something you like, dear."

Eddie took a step back. "What?"

"I found something in your room while I was tidying. It was an essay of sorts. About vampires being meant to bite and...other things."

"Fangs, Ma. I didn't write that. My buddy at work wrote it and handed it out to all the guys. I just hadn't thrown it away yet."

Judith sat down, landing on the stuffed flamingo with a squeak. Was it a dog toy? "Thank the stars!" she shouted.

I stood up. "I'm glad you two figured all that out, but Judith, you still purposely interfered with the police investigation."

"Huh?" Eddie asked.

He must have missed that part of the conversation, so I filled him on the fake hearts.

"So you're going to turn my mom in? Do you have any proof?"

"How else are the police going to figure out who got the real hearts? They need to inform the public to call in if they got a construction paper heart."

Eddie stepped closer to me. "You can just be vague, they don't need to know who—"

"No, Eddie," Judith said. "I'll tell them myself. I was trying to protect you, but since you aren't the culprit, I need to take responsibility."

He kept fighting with her but eventually backed down. "Fine. I don't like it, but if you feel the need to get yourself arrested, go for it. I gotta get back to work. I just came home to grab a blood bag."

With that, he stomped around in the kitchen before slamming the back door on his way out.

"You're doing the right thing," I told Judith. "Call the police now. I think the attacker will strike again very soon."

Chapter Twenty-Three

"How's everything going?" I asked Lacey while I warmed my hands on the van's vents.

"Just fine! The cake pickups are super easy. Hang on a sec." Her voice muffled, Lacey called out, "What was that, Dawk?" A few seconds later, her voice was clear again. "Sorry, Josie. Dawk says not to come back until you've got the attacker by the fangs."

I chuckled. "Tell him I'm trying. How's he doing?"

"He's trying to hide it, but he's on edge," she whispered. "A customer dropped a bone earlier, and Dawk dropped to the ground like we were doing World War II drills."

With a sigh, I said, "Thanks for keeping an eye on him."

"No problem. Except I really have to pee, but I don't want to leave him alone."

"Don't sacrifice your basic needs. Go to the bathroom, just be quick if you can."

"Okay!" The line cut off.

Laughing, I said to my empty car, "Bye to you too, Lacey."

I leaned back and adjusted the vents so they hit my face. It was only about noon, but the temperature had dropped to thirteen degrees. A light layer of snow covered the windshield, so I turned on the wipers, grateful that I didn't need to bust out my snow scraper yet.

Ruling Eddie out was easy, but before the attack last night, he'd been my only suspect. I had no idea who was responsible. All I had was my theory about the college.

Maggie was a student there. Dawk played soccer there. But what about Niall?

I took out my phone to call him. No answer. I left a vague message about having some follow-up questions. I texted him too.

Another attack was imminent. The culprit had been waiting a few days between attacks, but the game had changed after last night's failed attempt. Leaving the trinket indicated the attacker was moving on to another victim, which made sense. It would be too risky to go after Dawk again with all of us watching him so closely.

But was the next victim the last victim? Was Dawk's attack the penultimate scene of this violent play? Was the final scene coming soon? My gut told me it was.

Would the attacker wait until the middle of the night? Or would they attack some other time when their target was vulnerable, as they did with Dawk?

My phone rang, and a bolt of excitement shot through me. The number wasn't saved in my phone, but I still expected to hear Niall's voice on the other end.

Instead, I heard crunching.

"Erm, hello?" I asked hesitantly.

"Is this Josie Wixx?" a voice mumbled through the crunching.

"Yes. Who is this?"

A moment of pure crunching passed before they said, "This is Detective Craig."

"Oh! Thanks for calling. I take it you got my message."

Crunch. "Yep." Crunch. "And I just got a call." Crunch. "Your name came up." Crunch.

"Excuse me, are you eating something?"

"Potato chips—not that it's any of your business."

Ugh. From the thirty seconds we'd been talking, I already knew I wasn't a fan of Detective Craig, who must be human, given the potato chips. Vampires don't do potatoes.

"Okay, sorry, just asking," I said, trying to sound pleasant so he would keep talking to me. "Someone called you and mentioned me?" It must have been Judith.

"Yep, some woman told me she's been leaving paper hearts around town."

"I'm so glad she told you. I was—"

"She also said you'd been asking her and her son all kinds of questions," he interrupted. "Your name popped up on the statements from last night too."

"Yes, well—"

"I'm not sure what your deal is, but this is my case."

"Of course. But I'm a licensed private investigator, and I have every right to—"

He snorted. "Sure, you do, girl. Just don't get in my—"

"Do not call me girl, and stop interrupting me. I have every right to investigate. In fact, I just got Judith to admit that she was intentionally inferring with your case, so save your lecture for her. I need to talk to you about the trinkets left at each scene."

"Do you?"

"Yes. Please, just listen." I explained the significance of each trinket. Detective Craig didn't make a peep—except for the crunching, of course.

"So, you see, this new trinket that was left for me is about the next victim."

"How does that help us?" he asked, his tone mocking.

Wasn't that obvious? "Now that you know only the construction paper hearts are real, you can put out a notice to the town. Once you know who received real hearts, you can start puzzling out who is linked to the bird trinket."

"From what you've told me, the *trinkets*, as you called them, are pretty convoluted. It could take forever to piece all that together. We're better off increasing patrols and trying to catch the perp red-handed."

"Are you serious?"

"Very. I'll consider putting out a notice about the hearts, but the trinkets are useless. Now, stay out of my way." The line cut off.

"Bye to you too, Detective Craig."

He might think the trinkets were useless, but I knew better.

Feeling overwhelmed, I decided to take a break. With the storm coming, I needed to stock up on essentials—blood and wine.

Out for Blood was full of vampires with the same idea I had. The aisles were pretty tight in the bodega, so I had to raise my voice and poke a few vampires in the side to get my wheelchair through the crowd. I left with a heaping bag of blood.

I stored the blood in the van before rolling down Vein Street to The Bloody Grape. More people were out than I expected. Maybe some had left work early to prep for the storm.

Snow was falling faster now, accumulating on the brick sidewalk. It wouldn't be long before I'd have to send Zippy into hibernation until the storm was over and the sidewalks were clear again.

My friend Bayla was taking wine orders from a line of harried customers when I rolled into The Bloody Grape. I decided to stay for a bit. Most customers were rushing out the door, so I easily snagged my favorite booth by the window. I arranged the booth's cushy, dark-violet pillows to support my back and knees.

A waitress rushed up to take my order—three bottles of Lynnae's favorite wine-blood blend to go and a goblet of just blood to enjoy at the table. After she left, I pulled out my notebook.

Maggie. Niall. Dawk.

Dawk. Niall. Maggie.

Was there a pattern beyond each trinket revealing the next victim? Was Niall connected to the college campus somehow, like Maggie and Dawk?

I pulled out my phone to open Instagram. As long as we kept our accounts private and were careful with our posts, vamps could take advantage of social media.

After I'd met Niall, I'd requested to follow him. A goblet of blood appeared at my elbow just as I found Niall's account again. He'd approved my follow request.

With a long sip, I started scrolling. His posts were 90 percent random photos of things he saw throughout the day—an icicle on a bicycle, a bird with an injured wing, a beautiful beetle he'd seen last spring. The other 10 percent were photos with his wife, Shauna.

After ten minutes of scrolling, my fingers were starting to lock up. Hypermobile fingers aren't great for repetitive, fine movements. I was about to set my phone down and bang my head on the table when something caught my eye.

The post was another photo of Niall and Shauna, their eyes shining with the familiar gleam of alcohol consumption. They were both wearing black blazers, red shirts, and khaki pants. The post said that they'd dressed alike by accident, but told everyone at the event they'd done it on purpose.

Their clothes hadn't been what caught my eye, though. It was the carpet in the background. I knew that carpet. Navy with weird red and gold hexagons, the ugly carpet had burned itself into my brain back when I volunteered at various events in my college days.

Niall and Shauna stood in the executive ballroom at Arteria Falls College.

I chugged the rest of my goblet. Were they there for a one-time event, or did they have a more substantial connection to campus?

While I was deciding whether it was acceptable to call Niall every two minutes until he answered the phone, Bayla came over with my to-go bottles.

"Here you go, Josie. Oh, is that Niall and Shauna?" She grabbed my phone. "Niall is friends with my husband. It's a shame what happened to him. There's Wyatt in the background too. He comes in here sometimes. And look, there's Ronnie too."

I took my phone back before she could keep naming people in the background. "Niall is friends with your husband? Do you happen to know where he lives?"

She narrowed her eyes at me. "What are you up to, Josie Wixx?"

I laughed. "Nothing bad. I've been trying to figure out who's going around attacking vamps. Niall and I already met at the hospital. I need to talk to him again."

"Fine, but if he's creeped out by you showing up at his door, you didn't get his address from me."

Chapter Twenty-Four

A ddress in hand, I flew out the door a minute later, pausing only to zip up my coat and grab the bottles. The snow was really building. I had to very carefully wheel to the van.

"Sorry, Zippy," I told my chair as I lifted it into the van. "I think you'll be stuck in here for a while."

Niall lived in an adorable green two-story home. The combination of the cold and rolling through the snow had sent pain shooting through my body, so I took out my trusty tube of Bengay and doused my upper body before getting out of the car. Cane in hand, I approached the front door. A blue SUV sat in the driveway, so I hoped someone was home.

I rang the flamingo-free doorbell and waited. Hair mussed, Niall answered the door a few moments later.

"Josie?" he asked, understandably confused.

"Hi, Niall. I'm so sorry to drop by like this. I called earlier, but—"

"Oh, I was napping! Isn't that great? I get to nap in the middle of the day until I'm ready to go back to work." He waggled the fingers on his injured arm, which was secured in a sling. "Can't work if I can't type. Do you have more questions for me about the harrowing incident in which my blood was spilled like a red river of—"

"Niall, what are you going on about now?"

Shauna came down the hall carrying a striped dish towel, which she smacked against her husband's booty. "Are you glorifying your attack again?"

"Of course. How else am I supposed to process it? *Without* mockery and humor? No way."

Shauna, who wore a blue apron over an adorable knit lounge set, leaned in to kiss his cheek. "Right. How ridiculous would that be?" She must have been cooking, as tomato sauce had dribbled down the front of her apron. Tomatoes? Bleh. How humans eat those things, I'll never understand.

She turned to me, hand outstretched. "Hi! I'm Niall's wife, Shauna." As we shook hands, a tendril of brown hair escaped the clip on top of her head.

"I'm Josie. Niall answered some questions for me at the hospital."

"You must be the PI! What a cool gig." She pulled Niall away from the door—by his good arm, of course. "Come on inside."

She led us into a cozy living room full of books and beige furniture covered in a plethora of blankets. A black cat zipped out of the room.

"What's that smell?" Niall asked, sniffing in my direction.

I held my head high like I was some kind of royalty. "The glorious scent known to all humans and vampires of a certain age—Bengay."

He snickered. "It's quite glorious, indeed. Shauna, do you think we could get a Bengay-scented candle?"

She swatted him with the towel again. "You must be freezing, Josie. Would you like a heating pad?"

This woman was a saint. "That would be so amazing. I can't even tell you how amazing. Niall, it's a good thing you already married her because I would be proposing right now."

Laughing, she pulled a heating pad out of a basket and plugged it in for me. "Now, what can we do for you?"

I positioned the glorious heat over my knees and sighed. They'd been aching like crazy. "I'm working on a theory." I pulled my phone out of my coat pocket and showed them the Instagram post. "I found this photo of you two at the executive ballroom on campus. Do you go there often?"

"To the ballroom?" Niall asked with a raised eyebrow. "Just once a year for the admin awards."

"What about the rest of campus?"

"Only every Monday to Friday," Shauna said. "I work there."

I leaned forward in excitement. "You work on campus?"

She nodded. "Yes, I'm an admin for the Anthropology Department."

"Holy frickin' fangs. Are you serious?"

"No, she's lying to you, just for fun. Josie, what's going on?" Niall asked.

I tapped my fingers on the heating pad. "You all have connections to the campus. You, my cousin, Maggie."

"Your cousin?" Niall asked as his wife shot to her feet.

"Maggie? Maggie who?" she asked, her voice full of worry. I guess she wasn't logged into Roxie's Rumor Mill where somehow everyone knew about Maggie.

"Maggie Dodson."

"*Oh my stars.*" Shauna started pacing. "Maggie was the first victim? Is she okay? I'd heard it was a student, but that's it. I haven't talked to any of my university friends, though. I was out of town, and now, I've been off work taking care of Niall."

"I require hourly foot rubs," he explained.

Stifling a laugh, I caught Shauna's eyes. "Maggie's scared. The attack really spooked her. Physically, though, she's okay. Do you know her well?"

Shauna nodded, still pacing. "Yes. We're friends. I'm sure it sounds weird for a department admin to be friends with a student, but she spends a lot of time hanging around the office. She doesn't have a lot of friends."

"That was the impression I got." I rubbed my chin. "It's really weird that you're connected to both victims."

She came to a halt. "Wait, you don't think I have anything to—"

I cut her off by waving my hands. "No, I don't think you're involved. I'm just wondering if it's coincidental that you know both victims, or if that's somehow intentional."

"Why would it be intentional?" Niall asked.

I explained the significance of the trinkets. "So the culprit is pointing us to each victim, which is obviously a very intentional act. It makes me wonder if the connection to Shauna is intentional too."

"You said your cousin was attacked?" she asked, finally sitting back down. She sat very close to Niall now.

"Yes. Just last night. His name is Dawk." Shauna didn't appear to recognize his name, so I pulled up a picture of him.

She took a quick look. "I don't know him. How is he doing?"

Well, there went my theory that Shauna knew all the victims. "Dawk's okay. He's been staying with me, so the attacker couldn't get at him during the night. Instead, they attacked while he was getting in his car over on Magnolia after soccer practice. He was able to fight back and—"

"Hang on," Niall interrupted. "Did you say soccer? Does he play soccer at the campus rec center?"

"Yeah. A few nights a week."

"Josie," he said quietly. "I play soccer at the rec center."

"WHAT?" It was my turn to let surprise lift me to my feet. I longed to pace the floors as Shauna had, but my knees protested heavily, so I sat right back down. "You play soccer? On campus?"

"Yeah. Let me see the picture of your cousin." I held my phone out for him. "We aren't on the same team, but we play against each other sometimes."

"Fangs," I said. "So Maggie's connected to Shauna, who's connected to you, and you're connected to Dawk. And all of the connections revolve around the university."

"Do you think it's a student?" Niall asked.

I shrugged. "Maybe. Or someone else who works on campus or has another reason to spend time there."

"That's a lot of people," Shauna pointed out.

"Yep." I felt both exhilarated by these new developments and crushed by the idea that there were thousands of people on campus every day. "Is the attacker just weaving a web for fun? Choosing connected victims just because they feel like it? Or do they have a connection to each person?" I grabbed my notebook out of my other coat pocket. "Can you think of anyone on campus who has it in for you, Shauna?"

Both Shauna and Niall laughed. "Goddess, no," they said. Niall continued, "Everyone loves Shauna."

"I don't know about that, but I definitely don't have any enemies. I'm a people person."

"Hmm. Maybe it's someone who likes you *too much*. Anyone hit on you or otherwise give you unwanted attention?"

Niall stiffened. "If so, they better run once my arm is better because I'm going to beat—"

"Oh, hush, Niall. I can't think of anyone like that. Niall stops by the office frequently. Everyone knows we're married. Heck, at the admin awards every year, he runs around announcing himself as my husband and bragging about me to everyone, even my bosses." She gave him a stern look. "You better not do that this year because we've got a new Director of Central Administration. He's a huge jerk and won't like hearing about how good my coconut-lime blondies are."

He put a hand on his chest. "But it's my mission to tell the entire vamp world how amazing they are."

Wow, these two were possibly the most adorable couple I'd ever met. "Okay, so no enemies and no stalkers. Wait…stalkers…" I smacked my hand on my notebook and flipped back to my notes from Colleen. "Stalkers! Lunch tables! Shauna!"

"Umm, yes? I'm right here, Josie."

"I talked to another student in your department. Colleen? She told me Maggie sometimes ate with a department employee named Shauna, but I'd forgotten the name. Here it is, though," I said pointing at my notebook.

"Yep, I eat with her sometimes. We usually just gossip about the professors."

Bouncing my pen on the page, I said, "Shauna, I need you to think carefully. Does anyone ever watch Maggie while you guys eat?"

"Watch her?"

"Yes, from a distance."

She closed her eyes. "I don't know. I've never noticed anyone watching."

"Maybe you haven't noticed them watching, but maybe you've still seen them. Colleen told me a tall, pale man with sandy-blond hair watches Maggie. She said he's clean-shaven and wears khakis and polos." I checked my notes. "He also carries a duffel bag."

"That's like half the men on campus," Shauna said. "No one comes to mind right now, but I can try to think about it. Maggie hasn't noticed anyone?"

I shook my head. "Nope. Niall has my number if you think of anyone." I put my phone and notebook back in my pockets. "Thank you both so much. I have a lot to think about now."

Chapter Twenty-Five

After talking to Niall and Shauna, I couldn't see the whole quilt yet, but I could finally see part of the pattern. The college was at the core of this mess. Paper-Heartie knew enough about the victims to connect them all, stringing little paper heart banners between them, but where did the next banner lead? And what was the point?

None of the victims had any real enemies. They were too connected to be random. I doubted the attacker woke up one day and said, "What if I find a bunch of blonds with blue eyes and shove stakes in them? That would be fun."

No, there was something bigger going on.

I tapped on my steering wheel as I drove back to the boutique, trying to figure it out.

The attacker's identity felt so far out of reach. I knew they likely overheard my cousin discuss his Achilles tendinitis at the rec center. I knew Maggie's watcher carried a duffel bag, which implied participation in some kind of gym or sports activity. So I was ready to assume that the watcher was the attacker. He had the most boring description on the planet, though, so there wasn't a good way to narrow down his identity.

Colleen's words played in my head again. "*Tall, sandy-blond hair, pale, clean-shaven. Boring khakis and polos.*"

The blond hair was interesting. Maybe he'd always wanted lighter-blond hair and was taking out his frustrations on those of us he envied. The heart attacks were a lot of work for some hair envy, though. Like, just buy a box of bleach, dude.

He could be an employee, a student, or just someone who liked to hang around campus all day. I only had one idea to narrow down his identity.

The attacker had obviously taken great interest in his victims, so perhaps he'd followed them off campus too.

Pulling up to a stoplight, I grabbed my phone. "Willow, it's Josie," I said when the yoga teacher's voicemail kicked in. "I need your help. I need to know if a tall, pale, clean-shaven dude with sandy-blond hair has been coming to the yoga studio either during Maggie or Niall's classes. He has some kind of connection to the college if that helps. Please let me know!"

I had a hard time finding a parking spot on Vein Street. Everyone seemed to be picking up last-minute essentials before the storm hit. Luckily, the third time I circled around, someone pulled away from the curb in front of Isa's bakery.

Isa's was about to close. I thought about sneaking in for some coconut balls, but by the time I got out of the car with my cane, I'd seen three people enter my shop.

"Fangs, work is calling my name," I muttered to myself. "No coconut balls for this vampire."

I crossed the sidewalk slowly, making a mental note to grab the ice tip for my cane in case the snow turned to ice. Rubber and ice don't mix that well, so some genius inventor created pointy tips that slip onto rubber cane tips.

Having assumed business had only recently picked up in the boutique, I was surprised to see lots of people browsing and a line ten people deep. Lacey was asking people for the name on their cake receipt, while Dawk was on the register. A couple of people seemed to just want to grab their cakes and go, but most people were purchasing other goods, including lots of Valentine's Day toys.

"This is going to look great on Instagram next to Rocco's cake," a young vamp whispered to her friend, who didn't look so certain.

"I thought Rocco didn't really play with squeaky toys?" she asked.

Rocco's owner rolled her eyes. "So? My followers will love it."

Chuckling under my breath, I finally made it to the counter.

"Oh my stars, I'm so glad you're here!" Lacey's hair had become one massive tangle, and her eyes were huge. "He wouldn't let me call you! The town announced they were cutting all municipal employees early for the storm. Apparently, some of the other companies and the college decided to follow their example. It's been so busy!"

I grabbed her shoulders. "Take a deep breath. Let's do it together." I led her through two breaths. "Why don't you go out to the sales floor and see if anyone needs help? And check on Reggie, please?"

After she ran away, I turned to the crowd at the counter. "If you're just picking up a cake, step over here," I said, pointing to the far end of the counter opposite the register.

Three people came down. When they were gone, I sidled up next to Dawk and whispered, "You were supposed to call me if you got busy."

"Some things are more important, like our lives," he said through a big smile as he handed a woman her cake box and other purchases. "Have a fabulous day, ma'am!"

I gently moved him aside. "Can you grab my stool? The snow has trapped Zippy in the car, so I'll take over the register. You can round up cakes. Unless, of course, you'd rather help your best friend," I said, pointing down the line to where Tight-Bun was waiting with no less than five dog sweaters in her arms. "I bet she'll have lots of questions about those."

His face dropped, and he practically sprinted into the back to get my stool.

Matilda was hiding under the counter, looking adorable yet chic in a thick argyle sweater in three shades of purple.

Surprisingly, Tight-Bun only had ten or so questions about the sweaters. I'd expected thirty.

We fell into a good rhythm, Dawk and Lacey cycling between the sales floor and behind the counter, while I stayed plopped at the register.

Despite the crowd in the shop, I was somehow still cold, so in between customers, I dug under the counter for a heating pad I had stashed there.

Don't judge. It may seem unprofessional to use a heating pad at work but cold + pain = more pain, so it was necessary.

"If you think it's cold in here, don't go outside. It's down to nine degrees. The wind has picked up too," a familiar voice said.

Looking up, I recognized Sally's owner. "That must be why you have the world's puffiest coat on." I wasn't joking. His coat was huge. I thought his coat was thick the last time he came in, but this one was massive. I saw thick gloves sticking out of his pocket too. His beanie was of a normal size, though.

"I don't mess around when it comes to the cold. I should probably grow a beard to keep my face warm."

"They make these things called scarves. You may not have heard of them." He laughed as he set down the cans he held. "So you're back and buying six new types of cat food. I take it Sally didn't like any of the others?"

"You are correct. She's stayed far away from any chicken or beef I put down, but kind of licked a salmon one. I have high hopes for this salmon and shrimp concoction," he said, wagging one of the cans at me.

"That one is quite popular."

A minute later, he handed me a twenty, and I started to make change.

"I see you have a bird figurine on your bookshelf. Do you sell bird supplies here?"

Fangs. I'd forgotten about the bird trinket. With Detective Craig expressing zero interest in it, it was time to move it.

I looked behind his Stay-Puft-Marshmallow coat to check the line. No one was behind him. All the customers were still browsing, so I handed him his change and grabbed my cane. "Oh, this? I accidentally left it here earlier. It's my…errr…grandmother's. I need to return it to her. We don't even sell bird supplies—not enough space in here!" The figurine was smooth as I slipped it into my pocket.

"She's a fan of mockingbirds?"

My eyes widened. It was a mockingbird. "Erm. Yes. Big bird fan. Oh, I'm sorry, I have another customer."

"No worries. Stay safe out there, Josie."

I returned the sentiment, but I was barely paying attention. A mockingbird. Maybe it represented *To Kill a Mockingbird?* Was the next victim an English teacher?

The customers dwindled by four o'clock—probably snug in front of their fireplaces with hot chocolate. I was so jealous.

We only had a handful of cakes left. Lacey shooed me away from the counter when, due to a combination of achy hands and a distracted mind, I almost dropped one.

I dipped into the back, Matilda on my heels, and pulled out my phone. What else did a mockingbird represent?

Singing. Mimicking. Aggression.

Maybe a singing English teacher who mocks her students?

Ugh. I dropped onto a pallet of dog food, my thoughts spinning. Matilda jumped up to join me, burrowing into me for warmth.

Dawk found us there a few minutes later. "Holy fangs, Jos. That was crazy. We sold so much stuff. And now I'm exhausted." He plopped next to us.

"Same. You should have called me, but I did learn quite a bit while sleuthing today."

He sat up straight. "What? Tell me everything."

"Indulge me for a second first. Everly got a heart, right?"

"She got two hearts. Another one was on her front door when she left early this morning. She just told me earlier. I've been freaking out about it."

"Do you know what kind of paper they are? Construction paper or fancy paper?"

"Fancy paper. She showed me the first one the day she got it."

"Thanks the Goddess. I found out earlier today that only the construction paper hearts were left by the attacker. The fancy ones are decoys." I explained all about Judith's hearts and her suspicions about Eddie.

Dawk's shoulders, having been up near his ears for the past four days, finally relaxed a bit. "Bloody bite, I was so worried. I mean, I'm still worried about myself, but at least I don't have to worry about Everly anymore. What if they come back for me?"

I squeezed his shoulder. "I don't think they will. The attacker has to know we're watching you like a hawk now. It would be too risky. Keep being vigilant, but I really think they'll move on now." Especially since another trinket had appeared that morning.

Reaching into my pocket to pull out the mockingbird, I was about to tell him everything else that I'd learned, when his phone rang.

"It's Everly. Let me give her the good news." They gabbed for a couple minutes, Dawk telling her I'd concluded she wasn't a target. He turned to me. "Hey, Jos? Is it okay if I leave early? With the storm coming, we want to move up our Valentine's plans."

"Of course! This is the sixth day in a row you've worked. You're off the next three days anyway, so go start your time off early." He started to stand but I caught his wrist. "One more thing. Do you know a tall guy, pale, sandy-blond hair?"

"That doesn't ring a bell, but I know lots of guys through soccer. Wait, there's Darren." My heart started thumping. "You remember him? Super pale with a huge beard."

I sagged back down. "That's not him. This guy doesn't have a beard."

"Is it the attacker?"

"Yep. Keep an eye out for anyone of that description and let me know if you think of anyone who it could be."

"Will do."

He didn't hesitate to bundle up and flee into the storm, barely pausing to pat Matilda on the head. She, rightfully so, looked very offended.

I went back up front to find Lacey sweeping the floor. "How are you holding up?" I asked her.

"I'm okay! That was the busiest I've seen the store, but the time flew by." She gestured around the shop. "We have a lot of restocking to do."

My watch told me it was half past four. We still had an hour and a half left, but all the cakes were gone. "How about this? We clean and stock for the next thirty minutes and then close early."

Her face lit up. "That would be great. My roommates and I are doing a Galentine's Day! No boys, just wine and chocolate."

"That sounds amazing."

"Are you doing anything?"

My stomach flipped. The day's activities had been so distracting that I hadn't had a chance to freak out about my plans with Calder.

"Umm, yeah. Just hanging with a friend."

"A friend, huh? Your face is red, Josie. Like, burgundy."

"It's just hot in here."

She snorted. "It's freezing in here. The door is practically a sheet of ice."

I tapped my way to the front of the store, shivering as I got closer. The wind was howling, rattling the door and sending waves of cold inside. Poor Reggie was hiding in the farthest corner of his kennel. "Okay, let's get to cleaning so we can get out of here before the whole store freezes over. I don't want to leave Reggie here, though. What if he gets too cold? What if the storm gets so bad that we can't get here tomorrow?"

Lacey danced her way to his kennel. "I can take him home! My roommates will love him." She leaned down to coo at Reggie. "You'll be the only man allowed at Galentine's Day!"

One last customer came in to get a bag of dog food. By five, the streets were dead. Five inches of snow had already accumulated, and more was coming down. Fast.

My knees and ankles were killing me as we left the shop. Lacey carried Matilda to the van, not wanting her paws to get cold. She put the little Scottie on her seat in the back and covered her with a blanket we'd brought from the store.

"We can't have you getting cold, Matilda," Lacey told her.

Before locking up, I waited for Lacey to grab Reggie in the cat carrier I'd forced him into. If the scratches on my arms were proof, he wasn't likely to forgive me any time soon.

I drove Lacey and Reggie home, making sure they made it inside before Matilda and I pulled away.

"Let's go get ready for our not-a-date with Calder, girl!"

Matilda just burrowed further under her blanket, rudely ignoring me.

Chapter Twenty-Six

Lynnae left for her date with Alban at 6:00 p.m. sharp. He lived really close to us, so I was sure she'd be safe to make the drive, but I still told her to be careful.

Me? I was sitting in my favorite purple chair—the closet one to the door—and tapping my foot so much a hole must have been forming in the wood floor. Most days, I wore my hair down, but I wanted to change it up for my not-a-date. While I wasn't ready to date Calder, I still wanted to take his breath away. So before she left, Lynnae had helped me add flowing curls to my low side ponytail.

I'd applied red lipstick and sparkly gray eyeshadow too. I'd already had mascara on, but I'd added a few extra coats. It was too cold for a dress, so I'd opted for dark jeans that hugged my butt to perfection and a flowy purple top.

Now I was waiting for Calder to arrive in his Subaru. I couldn't take Zippy, so there'd been no point in trying to drive the van through the storm. Another couple inches had accumulated since I'd left the shop.

Thank goodness Arteria Falls had an excellent snowplow team.

Before my boot opened up the floorboards, Calder texted that he was outside.

I pulled on my coat, added a scarf, and pulled the hood tight. "Okay, Matilda, let's go!"

She lifted her head from beneath her pile of blankets for a second before burrowing in again.

"Aww, Matilda. I know it's cold, but I'm going to have you on my lap. C'mon!"

No movement.

I walked to her, using my crutch for support, and pulled off her blankets.

She blinked at me, her fluffy eyebrows twitching.

"I can't carry you to the car with one arm. I put your thickest coat on to keep you warm. You just have to hop down to Calder's car." I tapped over to the front door and grabbed her leash. "C'mon, girl! Do you want to go for a car ride?" Her tail twitched a smidge. "See, I know you want to go. Your buddy Calder is waiting!"

No movement.

I pulled out my phone to text Calder that Matilda had permanently attached herself to the couch. As I was contemplating dragging her off with my free hand, Calder let himself in.

Matilda jumped down, her tail a blur. She put her paws on Calder's legs and let out a bark.

"I missed you too, Matilda. Now let's go." He picked her up. She immediately snuggled up against his deep-blue scarf. "The car is warm, I promise."

Oh, my heart. A man who was smokin' hot and loved my dog? How I wished I could make him mine.

But things weren't that simple.

We made it to his house fifteen minutes later. He'd purchased a brick ranch a few years back. Much longer than it was wide, his house sat only a few feet from his neighbors on both sides.

Not long after we arrived, a roaring fire in Calder's gas fireplace warmed the living room. Freed from my outerwear, I pulled a thick crimson blanket over my legs. "This blanket is so soft, Cal."

"My mom sent it to me. I can ask her where she got it. Not that you need another blanket."

"Excuse me." I put my hand on my hip. "I *always* need more blankets. They're an essential aspect of my pain management plan."

"Mm hmm," he said, coming to sit next to me on the squashy gray couch. Matilda followed him, her head immediately finding his lap. "I'm sure your plan specifies dozens of blankets."

I gave him a little push. "It does. Now, what are we doing tonight?"

"I've got the blood blend ingredients—a bottle of Malbec, B+, pickles, and coconut water. Do you want to make the blend first or pick a movie?"

"How about we pick the movie?"

"Sure. Let's check Netflix." He bent forward to grab the remote. When he leaned back, he put his arm on the back of the couch. It was such a smooth move, so natural that my body responded on its own, scooting so close that my side ponytail rested on his shoulder.

I pulled my legs onto the couch cushion and bent them toward him. Rearranging the blanket, I asked, "Do you want under here?"

"Well, I don't, but I'm sure Matilda does," he said with a smirk.

I flopped the blanket over far enough to cover his legs and the little Scottie. "I guess you'll just have to suffer under the blanket to keep Matilda happy."

He laughed. "Worth it. What do you want to watch?"

As he scrolled through Netflix, I looked up at him. The room was dark, only the fire and the TV reflected in his eyes. His brown waves looked so soft that my fingers yearned to touch them.

Noticing my gaze, he met my eyes, the TV forgotten. A small smile brought his dimple to life, melting my heart. I didn't know what it was about that dimple, but it got me every time.

"You look so beautiful tonight, Josie." He brought a hand up to my ponytail. "I don't think I've seen your hair like this before. It suits you."

Note to self: wear hair in a curly side pony for the rest of my life.

"Thanks, Cal. My hair could never beat your perfectly mussed waves, though."

With a chuckle, he ran his fingers through said waves. "Growing up, my hair was frizzy and awkward, but I finally figured out how to squish a little product in after I shower."

Oh my stars, he actually used product on his hair. That was adorable. Was it as soft as it looked, or would the product make it a bit stiff?

I'd resisted for years, but my fingers couldn't wait any longer. Calder looked surprised as I lifted my hand. Pausing, I looked into his eyes, searching for permission. He nodded, so I gently ran my fingers over his hair before letting them dive in. His tresses indeed were soft. So soft.

He let out a deep sigh. A sigh of longing, of relief. "That feels so good."

When I pulled away, Calder was looking at me so tenderly that I knew we'd finally reached *the moment*. Maybe because it was Valentine's Day, maybe because

I was sick of denying myself what I so clearly wanted, or maybe it was my grandmother's words echoing in my mind, *"You know, Josie, those who love us, love us. All of us."* Whatever the reason, when he reached for my hand, I didn't pull away.

"Josie, I—"

Brrrrrnnggggggg

"Fangs!" I reached across the coffee table to grab my purse. "I'm so sorry. I left the ringer on in case Willow calls me back about the case, but it's probably just my mom." I dug past random receipts and three tubes of Bengay to find my phone at the bottom. "Oh! It is Willow."

I gave him a pleading look.

"It's okay, Jos. Answer it." I squeezed his forearm.

"Hey, Willow! I take it you got my message."

"Yep! I was prepping for my girlfriend to come over, sorry. We're making a plaster mold of our hands tonight!"

I dug my fingernails into my palm, resisting the urge to tell her I didn't care. "That's so cool! I bet that's messy. So, anyway, about the man I mentioned in my—"

"Yes! There's a guy who started coming to Niall's class about a month ago or so that fits that description. He's super nice. His downward dog needs a lot of work, but he has a lot of potential. He's the one who helped me break up the fight between Niall and Eddie."

My heart jumped into my throat. This had to be the guy. "Do you know his name?"

"I do. We always chat a bit after class. His name is Wyatt. I have a discount program for employees or students at the college. Wyatt always flashes his ID card at me to get the discount, so I'm guessing he's your guy."

Wyatt. Where had I heard that name?

"Willow, do you know whether he's a student or an employee?"

"Employee. It's in big letters on the ID. He's too old to be a student too. I'd say in his forties."

"Do you know anything else about him? His last name? Where he lives?"

Voice full of regret, Willow told me, "No, I'm sorry. Even if I was willing to share private information on my clients, he never mentioned where he lives. I didn't pay attention to his last name. He always pays cash too, so I don't have any credit card records for him either."

A pang of disappointment shot through me, but at least I had a first name and an age. That was huge.

"I can't tell you how helpful this is. I owe you another blend at The Bloody Grape."

"Don't worry about it. I'm happy to help. Do you think Wyatt knows something about the attacks?"

"You could say that. I have to go, Willow. Thanks so much."

I hung up to find Calder and Matilda staring at me.

"Cal, I've got his name. Wyatt. He's in his forties and works on campus. Sandy-blond hair. Tall. No facial hair." I filled Calder in on the day's developments, everything from the fake hearts to Shauna and Niall to Detective Craig's imbecility.

He let out a soft whistle. "You've made a lot of progress today. Now how do we find Wyatt?"

Wyatt. Wyatt. Wyatt. The name spun through my brain.

"Holy fangs." I grabbed Calder's hand. "I remember where I heard that name today."

With my free hand, I navigated back to Niall's Instagram post in the executive ballroom. "Bayla listed names of people in the background. Wyatt was one of them."

I zoomed in, moving around the photo. "Dracula's cape," I whispered, my phone falling from my fingers, the blood draining from my face.

Calder picked it up, quickly finding the blond man in the background. "What is it, Jos? Do you know this guy?"

"I just talked to him a couple of hours ago. About mockingbirds."

Chapter Twenty-Seven

I pulled the mockingbird out of my pocket and set it on the coffee table.

Was Wyatt mocking me with the little bird figurine, pointing me at his next victim, or both? He'd clearly come into Matilda's VamPets just to play with me.

The rec center, the yoga studio, watching Maggie, my shop—this guy was everywhere. He'd probably come in the first two times to observe Dawk, using the story about his new cat as a cover. Did Sally even exist?

That day, though, he'd come for me.

I thought back to our encounters over the last few days. Wyatt's hair was under a beanie the last two times I saw him, so I hadn't realized he'd had the sandy shade I was looking for. His first visit, his head was bare, but I'd forgotten all about that. He'd been just one customer among so many.

Wyatt had been beyond polite. Even rather charming. He didn't seem like the type to go on a biting and staking spree, but isn't that what you hear in every true crime documentary? The culprit never seems like the type.

Calder had been waiting patiently while I processed everything. I filled him in on Wyatt's visits to the shop.

"How do we find the next victim, though?" I asked. "It's been hours, and no message has gone out on the town app about the construction paper hearts." I curled my fingers into a fist. "I can't believe Detective Craig didn't notify the town."

"Maybe he thinks the snowstorm will keep everyone inside, even the attacker."

I snorted. "Or it gives him good cover. No one outside to see him skulking around."

Wyatt would move for checkmate any second. Why else would he come into my store and comment on the very trinket he left? Why else tell me it was a mockingbird? Why else leave me the knight piece?

"Maybe you should call Shauna. He was in the background at her awards banquet, so she might know him."

I snapped my fingers. "You're right. Let's do it."

Putting my phone on speaker, I called Niall.

"Josie! I hope you're home and snuggled up by a fire with a massive wine goblet."

I laughed. "Well, I am by a fire, just not at my house."

"Oooooooh, are you at a paramour's house on this fine Valentine's evening?"

Regretting the speaker setting, I laughed off his comment, but I could feel a blush creeping up my neck. I shook it off. "Niall, I hope I didn't interrupt a romantic night with Shauna, but I really need to speak with her."

"No problem." His voice muffled, he called out, "Yo, hunny buns, Josie needs to talk to you."

"Hold your vampire bats, I'm taking some blondies out of the oven," Shauna called back.

"Josie, you'll have to wait. My wife is in the middle of the most sacred task known to vampires—baking with the, like, three ingredients our people can eat."

Calder snickered beside me, loud enough for Niall to hear. "Oh? Is that the paramour? Hi, there. I'm Niall. I like long walks through the forest, fresh blondies, and—"

"Give me that," we heard before a kerfuffle of friction came down the line. "Sorry about him, Josie. He's so ridiculous," she said, her voice full of love. "What can I help you with?"

"There's been a development," I began. "Do you know someone named Wyatt?"

"Yep. He's an admin over in the English department. Why?"

"Have you ever seen him floating around the pavilion where Maggie eats?"

"Maybe? I see him out and about on campus fairly often, but I don't remember when or where." She paused. "Josie, are you saying Wyatt is behind the attacks?"

I sighed. "I think so. He's been coming into my shop—where my cousin works—and attending Niall's yoga classes."

"Wait, what?"

"It's true. Willow, who owns the yoga studio, told me about him. Then I found him in the background of your awards banquet photos."

"Hang on, I'm putting Niall on the line too." She switched to speaker and told him about Wyatt. "I think you met him a couple times at the admin awards."

"I meet a lot of people at those events."

"Let me pull up a picture," Shauna said.

A second later, Niall said, "Fangs. I recognize him. He's the one at yoga who got between me and that jerk who ogles women."

Willow had said the same thing.

Disbelief apparent in her voice, Shauna said, "That doesn't mean he's behind the attacks, though. Yoga is a common hobby. Shopping at a pet store is a common activity. Maybe it doesn't mean anything."

"It's more than that, though. He was just in my shop earlier, and while I didn't realize it at the time, I see now that he was taunting me. I found the next trinket, a little bird, in my shop this morning. I left it where it was. Wyatt pointed it out to me. He told me it was a mockingbird."

"Maybe he just knows about birds," she said.

I bit my lip. "Look, I know it must be hard to think someone you know attacked your husband. If I'm wrong, then Wyatt will be fine and I can keep searching. But if I'm right, we need to stop him before he attacks again. I have a bad feeling about the next attack."

Shauna let out a heavy breath. "You're right. How can I help?"

"What's Wyatt's last name?"

"Curran."

Wyatt Curran. Finally, a full name.

"Can you think of anyone he has an issue with?"

"Well, we aren't close friends, so I don't know that much about him. Let me think." A few seconds passed before Shauna gasped. "There is someone. We have a new Director of Central Administration. Each admin is responsible to the professor who heads their department, but we technically work under the DCA. We have to do all our paperwork a certain way, send through specific reports about finances, etcetera."

"And Wyatt hates him?" I asked. Was this guy the next victim?

"We all do, but…it's different with Wyatt. He's usually nice, laid back, charming. I figured he'd be the first admin to approach the new director, but at every meeting we have, he hides in the back. I didn't think too much of it. The new director is overbearing, demanding, and even aggressive sometimes, so it made sense that Wyatt wanted to stay away from him.

"But Wyatt and I were talking after we bumped into each other on the way to our cars. He told me he thinks Jack is the worst thing to happen to Arteria Falls College. He wasn't showing signs of anger so much as hatred. His eyes were so dark. His lip curled. It was like he thinks Jack is evil or something."

Fangs. I recognized that name. "Shauna, how new is Jack?"

"Just a couple of months."

Calder squeezed my leg. "What are you thinking?"

"I think I've met Jack."

Chapter Twenty-Eight

"**G**rr. Answer the phone, Dawk!"

I threw my phone on the couch. I'd hung up on Shauna with a quick promise to keep her updated and immediately dialed my cousin. I'd called three times already. He was probably making out with Everly.

"Josie, why are you calling Dawk? Who's Jack?"

I collapsed in on myself, head in my hands. "Everly's father."

"What the fangs? Are you sure?" Calder asked.

"A few days ago, he came into the shop to yell at Dawk. Jack was rude, aggressive, unreasonable. He thought Dawk was putting Everly in danger because he'd received hearts, but Everly had received one too. Earlier today, Dawk told me the first heart she got was the fancy paper. I remember Dawk mentioning a second heart had appeared, but I assumed it was another fancy heart for Everly. Now I'm thinking it was for Jack. If it was construction paper, he's our next victim."

I sat back up and used my fingers to keep track. "He fits the victim profile physically, Wyatt loathes him, and he just moved here. This whole investigation I've wondered *why now?* Jack's appointment to director could have set all of this off."

Calder leaned back. "He created this whole intricate plan just because he hates his boss?"

"I don't know. It does seem weird. Maybe he's been wanting to pull off an attack scheme for a while and his hatred for Jack set him off. Wait!" I grabbed his hand and squeezed. "I just remembered that Wyatt was in the shop when Jack came in to yell at Dawk. Jack ran right into him and didn't recognize him. Wyatt froze up and just stared at Jack. I thought maybe he was making sure Jack wasn't going to hurt me, but maybe he was just…wallowing in his hatred of Jack."

Calder squeezed back. "It all fits, Josie. You need to call Detective Craig. He seems useless, but he needs to know."

"Ugh, fine." I grabbed my phone, but he didn't answer. I left a message. "Why does no one answer their phones!?"

It seemed prudent to call Dean, the police contact I'd developed, as well. After a minute of talking to him, it became clear he wasn't going to be any help.

"Joooossie. Why does Valentine's Day exist? Is so stupid. Like really stupid. Jooooossssie. Do you wanna come over? I have, like, looots of wine. Maybe not as much as I had an hour ago, but is still aaaaa loooootttt. Did I ever tell you how purdy you are?"

Calder could clearly hear Dean, as he took my phone and hung it up. I hoped Dean wouldn't remember talking to me, because that was embarrassing for the both of us.

I called Dawk two more times before he finally answered. "Josie," he whispered as if he didn't want to be caught on the phone. "I'm a little busy."

"Yeah, well, this is more important. I need you to ask Everly two questions about her dad."

He groaned. "I don't want to bring up her dad on Valentine's Day."

"Dawk," I said, my voice rigid. "I think he might be the next victim."

"Dracula's cape. Let me get her." A moment later, Everly was on the line.

I took a deep breath. "Everly, Dawk told me a second heart showed up at your house. Was it made out of construction paper?"

Her voice was higher than normal when she replied. "Yes. Two construction paper hearts showed up. One was left overnight or really early this morning. The other one showed up this afternoon."

Fangs. "Okay, thanks. Does a bird figurine, specifically a mockingbird, have any association with your dad?"

"Umm, yes. He's a huge birder. He goes out every weekend morning to look at birds. It's so lame."

I looked at Calder. Still holding my left hand, he ran his thumb over my palm and nodded. With a huge breath to steady myself, I said, "Everly, I think your dad is in danger from the attacker. Where is he right now?"

"What!? But how do you know? Practically all the blonds in town received hearts."

"I know, but my investigation has led me to your dad. We need to move quickly. Where is he?"

Breathing hard, she said, "He's still at work. The department is a mess, so he's been working late every day. My dad refuses to celebrate Valentine's Day, so tonight's no different. He wouldn't even leave early because of the storm. My mom tried."

I stood up. "So he's alone on campus. I need you to call him. Keep calling until he answers. Tell him to be careful and not to go wandering around."

"I'll tell him, but he might not listen. He won't believe the attacker can actually hurt him. He'd just try to fight them off and assume he can win."

Jack did seem like the type for fight not flight. "Just try. I'll call the detective again."

Fetching my coat, I signaled to Calder to put his on too. Knowing I couldn't be talked down, he didn't even hesitate to grab his coat.

"Can we leave Matilda here?" I asked.

"Of course."

I kissed her goodbye, Calder killed the fire, and we were off.

Chapter Twenty-Nine

"What could Detective Craig be doing that's so important he isn't answering his phone? The desk officer told me his desk phone goes through to his cell phone."

"Maybe he has a hot date," Calder joked.

"Ha. It's hard to imagine someone as difficult as him could be on a date, but anything's possible."

I put my phone in my pocket. Dawk texted that Everly hadn't been able to reach her dad, but she'd keep trying. He was supposed to call me if she connected with him. Dawk had wanted to come to campus to find him, but Everly melted down after we got off the phone. Worried for her dad, she'd been crying and hyperventilating.

So it was just me and Calder.

"What if Jack's not answering his phone because Wyatt already got to him?"

I groaned. "I really hope that's not the case, but we need to prepare for the possibility. What building is Central Administration in?" I asked.

"Crowley. Their offices are right next to Human Resources."

I nodded. Crowley was on the far side of campus, away from the dorms, student union, and most of the academic buildings. The area would likely be empty.

Mercifully, though, Crowley was right next to a parking garage. Considering most of the uncovered spaces were covered in several inches of snow, parking in one would have been difficult.

"Josie, I think you need to wait here," Calder said as we pulled into the garage. "The college cleared the sidewalks earlier, but three more inches of snow have accumulated since then. There could be ice underneath the snow too."

"The building's not that far." I pointed across a small clearing. "I'll be okay. I've got the ice tip on the bottom of my crutch. Jack doesn't know you at all. We've at least met, so I hope he'll listen to me."

He pulled into a space on the lowest level. "True, but he sounds generally uncooperative."

"What if Wyatt sees me over here? Or sees you coming and attacks you? I really feel like we need to stick together. It's not like you can get over to the building that fast right now anyway. As you said, there could be ice."

His jaw ticked for a second before his face fell. "Okay, let's go."

Ice, indeed, had formed after the sidewalks were cleared earlier. Each step required my full attention. Calder kept his hand on my non-crutch arm, but luckily, I didn't need him to catch me. Thank you, ice tip.

A couple sets of tracks led in and out of Crowley. I hoped none of them were Wyatt's.

Buildings that weren't for student use typically locked automatically around 7:00 p.m., so Calder had to use his key card to get in. Had Wyatt thought of that? If he attacked here, the log would show his entry.

No sounds met our ears inside Crowley. The lights were off. Beams trickling in from outside were all we had to light the way.

I leaned on Calder to pull the ice tip off my crutch. Not wanting the wet crutch to squeak on the linoleum floors, I tried to dry the bottom on the rug by the door.

"Which way?" I whispered.

"Down the hall, to the left."

The cold had edged its way into my joints. Every step was agony, but I'd grown used to ignoring pain.

Light shined through an office window when we turned the corner. Calder pointed at it and nodded. This must be our destination.

We pushed ourselves against the wall and slid along it. "The door is slightly cracked," Calder said. Did someone forget to close it all the way, or had Wyatt left it open for a quick exit?

He leaned over, peering through the window. "The light is coming from the very back room. I can't see inside it, though."

I nodded. We'd decided on the walk over that Calder would go in first. He wouldn't have it any other way. Before he could go in, I grabbed his elbow and pulled him into a side hug. He squeezed me hard.

The door labeled *Central Administration* was quiet as he opened it, no squeaks betraying his entry. I squeezed my fingernails into my palms and sent a prayer to the Goddess that he would be safe.

Leaning over, I watched him walk down a short hall toward the light.

With slow movements, he approached the room at the back. I saw the moment his shoulders relaxed, mine following suit. He knocked on the door.

I heard a gruff voice answer him, but my ears tuned them out as soon as a cold object pressed against the back of my head.

Fangs.

"You're quite the detective, Josie Wixx," Wyatt said.

"You too, Wyatt. You seem to know everything, including my last name."

He stepped close enough for me to feel his puffy coat brush against my much-less-puffy one. "I'm a good researcher."

"Do you even have a cat?" I hoped not. No kitties deserved to live with this ball of bonkers.

"Nope. Now, don't move. No fangs, either."

My fangs had snapped down as soon as I'd felt him behind me, so I pulled them back in. I didn't want to get shot because my fangs were out.

"Is that a gun or your fireplace poker?" I asked, my voice bitter.

Wyatt laughed. "Very funny. I left the poker at home tonight."

My heart started pounding. Guns aren't sold in the vampire world. They just never took off with us. Maybe because we've never had a reason to hunt animals. Wyatt must have driven to the human world at some point. I guess I was right that he didn't want to take chances with Jack. You can't fight off a gun as easily as a fireplace poker.

"Here's what's going to happen. You're going to open that door and tell your friend you're coming in. If you mention me or the gun, I'll shoot you."

I didn't move. "Really? You haven't caused any permanent damage to anyone yet. Why would you shoot me?"

"Other than because you know who I am?"

Good point. I eased forward, leaning heavily on my crutch. My poor legs weren't enjoying holding me up for so long.

"Calder, I'm coming in."

I walked slowly, trying to figure out what the fangs to do. I *could not* let Calder get hurt.

His voice was full of frustration as he called back, "Okay, Jos."

I could hear his conversation with Jack now. It was *tense*. Apparently, Jack's work number went to his cell phone, which was on silent, so he hadn't heard Everly calling either number. He wasn't impressed by our investigation, and as Everly had predicted, claimed he could fight off "this motherfanger stabbing people with pencils."

When I got near Jack's office, I whispered to Wyatt, "What now?"

He put his arm around my chest, resting it on my collarbone, and pulled me into him.

Tossing my crutch aside, he turned us sideways and dragged me into the office, his gun held out in front of him.

Chapter Thirty

"**S**tay where you are. Keep your fangs in your gums," he said calmly.

Jack's office was bigger than I'd expected. A sleek black couch sat on one wall, a massive square coffee table in front of it. A large window looked out over the snowy night. Calder was standing across from Jack, his arms crossed.

Both men froze, staring at us.

Jack recovered first. "You look familiar."

"I should hope so," Wyatt said.

"Not you," Jack said. "Her."

Wyatt pulled me tighter. "Her cousin is dating your daughter."

"Oh, yeah. You're the chick from the pet shop."

I rolled my eyes. It was my absolute favorite when men called me a *chick*. "I think you mean the *woman* from the pet shop."

"Shut up, both of you," Wyatt ordered. He pointed the gun between Calder and Jack. "Put your hands up."

Both men listened, thank the stars. If Jack decided to resist, he could get us all killed.

Wyatt pushed me forward. I wasn't ready for it and my right knee buckled. Calder started to step forward, but I held my hand out to stop him. His jaw tightened, but he stayed put.

The door click closed behind Wyatt. "What's your friend's name, Josie?"

"You don't know it? I thought you were a *good researcher*."

"Your friends didn't seem important. Why did you involve someone else, anyway?"

My stomach clenched. Oh, how I wished I hadn't involved him. "His name is Calder. Hurt him, and I'll make sure every bone in your body breaks."

"Right," Wyatt said, voice full of sarcasm. "You seem capable of that."

"Don't test me," I said through gritted teeth.

He waved the gun around. "I think it's you who shouldn't test me. Now sit on the couch."

After he released me, I crossed to the couch as quickly as possible, desperate to get off my legs. The pain in my knees eased, but my back muscles twisted.

"Sit next to her," he told the men.

Wyatt had come prepared with thin but dense red rope, pulling it out of a satchel he'd draped across his body. He made Calder tie up Jack's hands and feet, made me tie up Calder, and had me tie my own feet. He pulled on all the knots to check them.

He left my hands free, seemingly to avoid setting the gun down to tie them himself. I guess, as he said, I wasn't *capable* enough to be a threat.

"That's better. Now we can talk." He sat on the desk, his puffy coat knocking over a pen cup.

"*We* can talk, or *you* can talk?" Jack asked.

Wyatt smiled. "You and I can talk. These two have nothing to do with this. You seriously don't recognize me?"

Jack huffed. "No. This guy," he tilted his head toward Calder, "told me one of my employees was after me." He ran his eyes over Wyatt's face. "I can't be expected to know all my admins."

Wyatt sat the gun down and took off his satchel and coat. "Actually, I think you should know all of us. There are a lot of admins, but so what? Take the time." He crossed his arms. "That's not the only reason you should know me, though."

So Jack wasn't just Wyatt's boss? That made more sense. This whole scenario had been too elaborate for just hating your boss.

Wyatt's nostrils flared. "Maybe this will remind you." Picking up the gun, he walked to the couch and stuck his face just inches from Jack's. "Any of these fun names sound familiar to you? Wimpy Wyatt? Funky Fangs? You convinced our whole grade to hold their noses when they looked at me."

Jack's eyes lit up in recognition. "Oh, yeah. I remember you now. Wyatt Curran. My favorite was actually Curvy Curran, you know, cause you used to be so f—"

Wyatt slapped Jack so hard his fangs snapped down.

"Every. Single. Day. You taunted me every day. Putting your evil blue eyes right in my face. You mocked everything I said. You even rode your bike by my house after school and on the weekends just to bully me. I had nightmares about your vicious eyes every night."

So that was their connection. Dawk had told me Everly's family used to live here, but it hadn't occurred to me that Jack had known Wyatt before they left.

I closed my eyes for a second. As much as I didn't want to, I felt bad for Wyatt. I couldn't imagine the pain of being bullied every day.

Jack showed no remorse. "Some people are strong. Some people are weak. I didn't make you weak. Blame your mother for—"

SMACK.

This time, Jack's head bounced off the back of the couch.

"Who's weak now? When I saw your ugly face for the first time after you took over as director, I knew you hadn't changed. You were so smug during your little introduction speech."

Wyatt crossed back to the desk. "I thought I'd gotten rid of you when you left Arteria Falls all those years ago. If you had stayed away, none of this would have happened."

"Even the other attacks, Wyatt?" I asked.

He flattened his lips. "When I saw Jack again, I realized how many other people with those same eyes, that same hair had wronged me. I tried to run off my frustration at the track every day, but my anger only increased. So I embraced it and started planning my revenge. I thought it would be fun to play a game." He clenched his fists. "Someone got in the way, though. Whoever left those fake hearts messed things up. I wanted Jack to know he was a target. I wanted him looking over his shoulder like I did for all those years."

"How did the others hurt you?" Calder asked.

Jack turned to Calder. "Does it matter?" More quietly he said, "Look the two of us can take him, we just have to—"

Wyatt banged the gun on the desk. "Don't even think about it. All this talk is getting old." He looked around.

"I need to figure out where to put each of you. I didn't bring enough hearts," he mumbled.

I bumped Calder's shoulder while Wyatt was distracted. When he looked at me, I pointed one finger at my feet.

Grandpa Roan taught me a lot over the years. Not just how to investigate, but how to fight, how to escape. How to tie all kinds of knots, including escapable knots.

Moving quickly and thanking the Goddess for the huge coffee table in front of us, I moved my feet in just the right way to disengage the knot. The ropes still sat on my boots, but I was free.

Calder mimicked me. He was smart enough to leave his hands, which would have been too easily noticed by our captor.

Jack hadn't been paying any attention to us. He'd been tugging on his hands in a way that actually tightened the knots.

A couple seconds later, Wyatt refocused on us. "The three of you should fit on the floor no problem."

"Wyatt," I said, my voice soft. "What Jack did to you is awful. Inexcusable. I understand why you want to hurt him back. But they'll know this was you. Your key card will show up on the security log."

"You think I can break into houses and your shop but not this building? The mechanism is different, but it's not that sophisticated."

I took a deep breath, preparing to be slapped myself after my next revelation. "I left a message for the detective assigned to this case. He knows who you are already."

To my surprise, he only shrugged. "I knew they'd figure it out eventually. Don't worry about me. There's a sweet spot in the human world calling my name. I'll just have to get out of town faster than I'd planned."

"What about me and Calder? We haven't done anything to you. You're just going to kill us too?"

"You know, I actually like you. You're funny. But I won't feel too bad about taking you out, considering..." he trailed off, his eyes flicking to my hair. "Your friend here isn't my fault either. It was your choice to involve him."

My phone rang then, scaring the veins out of me. Was it Detective Crabby, finally calling me back? I could only hope he'd listened to my voicemail and taken me seriously. Maybe the police were on their way.

Snow was quite an obstacle, though. It was coming down so hard I could barely see six inches past the window.

We had to get out of this ourselves.

Narrowing my eyes at the window, I said, "Oh, thank the Goddess. The police are here."

Chapter Thirty-One

The lie had done the trick. Wyatt pivoted to the window, squinting for the nonexistent police.

Not wasting a second, I flipped the coffee table onto its side and pulled the ropes off my feet. Jack tried to jump up, but the ropes toppled him straight over the coffee table, putting him closer to Wyatt.

Wyatt flipped around, trying to decide where to point his gun. It landed on Jack, so I reached over and freed Calder's hands. The two of us dove behind the coffee table.

"Stop moving!" Wyatt shouted.

My eyes met Calder's. I tapped the coffee table. "I'll throw it. You get him." I might have been weak for a vampire, but I was strong enough to throw a coffee table, even this monstrosity. I knelt and whipped the table at Wyatt.

With a crash, it sent him sailing into the window. Calder zoomed after the table and pinned it against Wyatt. His gun hand was still floating around, though. Full of adrenaline, I zipped over and slammed his hand against the window.

The gun went off, shattering the window behind Wyatt. All three of us and the coffee table toppled through.

Snow and glass broke our fall, a piece of the latter slitting open my cheek.

The table had shifted, and Wyatt tried to wriggle free. He still had the gun, but I still had his arm. Since he'd removed his stupidly oversized coat, his skin was vulnerable.

So I bit him. I didn't even snap my fangs down. We were allowed to bite in self-defense, if absolutely necessary, but a human-level bite was enough to get him to drop the gun. Besides, my fangs were way too good for him.

I grabbed the gun and rolled to the side. Wyatt tried to sit up, but Calder punched him, knocking him out.

"Good job, Cal. Give him a taste of his own medicine."

Breathing hard, he smiled. "I should have used a fireplace poker."

I laughed and tried to stand, but my legs were too shaky, so I just collapsed into the snow, luckily away from any glass. My poor ponytail, so expertly curled, instantly soaked up the snow.

Calder stood and moved the coffee table to the side. "Let's tie him up."

A few minutes later, Wyatt was tied up with his own ropes, Jack was untied, and I was incessantly calling Detective Craig.

"This better be good, Josie," he said when he finally deigned to answer.

"Hey, buddy! Can I call you 'buddy'? You knew it was me, so you must have saved my number in your phone. I'm flattered." Pouting, I continued, "Or maybe I shouldn't be since you've been ignoring me all night!"

"Get. To. It."

"Seeing as we're friends, I thought I'd help you out, Detective Craig. I've found you a man. He's about six foot three with sandy-blond hair and—"

"Josie!"

I dropped the act. "I found the next victim. And I found the culprit. He was going to kill me, my friend, and his intended victim. Basically, I did your job, and because you ignored me, I was in danger. My friend was in danger. So please get your butt over here and arrest this guy."

He hadn't even listened to my message earlier, so I had to fill him in on where we were. With the snow, it would be a while, so we waited.

Jack and Calder lifted Wyatt back into the office. As tempting as it was, we didn't need him getting hypothermia on our watch.

Once he was deposited on the floor, Jack collapsed into his desk chair, going completely silent.

After Calder went to prop the building's door open for the police, he and I huddled together on the couch, both freezing from the snow and the cold seeping into the room. We never took our coats off, but it was still frickin' frigid.

Every few seconds, I looked at my couch buddy to remind myself he was still there. Calder never should have been in this situation. The longer we sat there, the guiltier I felt. I was the one investigating. I was the one with training. Calder had handled himself well, and he hadn't been hurt, but he *could have been*.

A world without Calder was an unacceptable world.

Interrupting my self-loathing, Wyatt moaned and sat up.

"Fangs," he said, taking in the ropes.

Full of fury, I didn't hold back. "How does it feel? Is being tied up everything you imagined? What about being hit in the head? Do you think this is how Maggie felt when she woke up covered in blood? You said you wanted Jack to be paranoid, to have to look over his shoulder like you had to as a kid. Did you want that for

Maggie too? Because that's what's in store for her now. A life of fear."

Wyatt furrowed his brow. "She should have thought of that before she rejected me."

I snorted. "It seems like she made the right decision. How long had you been stalking her at lunch before you made a move?"

He didn't respond.

"Quite some time then? So she rejected you. What about Niall?"

Wyatt looked like he wasn't going to answer, so I said, "Was your problem even with him, or was it with Shauna?"

His face reddened. "It was with him! He went around bragging about her, joking about her. Making it clear she was his. He didn't deserve her."

I snorted. "That's ridiculous. Shauna and Niall seem to have a great relationship."

"Shut up! You don't know what you're talking about. He's awful. When I was in his yoga class—"

"Stalked him to his yoga class."

"—he got in a fight with some dude. He was so aggressive."

"Which, combined with the hair and eyes, reminded you of Jack."

Wyatt nodded, a vein in his neck pulsing.

"Okay, but why on earth did you choose my cousin? He's a sweetheart. There's no way he offended you."

Seething, Wyatt looked at Jack. "Your cousin was dating his daughter. Anyone who would associate themselves with—"

He didn't get a chance to finish. A heavy hole puncher flew at his face, knocking him out again. Jack had had enough.

We sat in silence until wet footsteps squeaked down the hall.

When Detective Craig, who looked exactly like I expected—short and balding with a pinched face—walked through the door, I gave him a gleeful look.

"Oh, yay! You've arrived. Here's your Valentine's Day present, all nice and wrapped up in red ribbons."

He was not amused.

Chapter Thirty-Two

Two days later, my body was a living manifestation of the fires of hell.

Okay, that might be a tad dramatic. More like a four-alarm fire. Everything hurt, from a massive headache to swollen ankles and everything in between.

After Wyatt had been carted away, Calder and I had picked up Matilda. The storm had raged as we'd inched through town in the Subaru. We'd eventually made it to my house, where I'd collapsed onto my bed, barely managing to get my coat off first. Matilda had curled up on my head like a cat. I'd made Calder promise to text me when he'd arrived home safely. As soon as I'd received his text, my eyes had closed. For sixteen hours.

When I'd pried myself out of bed in the late afternoon yesterday, I'd felt like I'd been run over by a car, then a truck, then a bus, followed by a freight train. I'd shoved my meds down and crawled back between the sheets, praising my heated mattress pad.

Now, it was 10:00 a.m. on the sixteenth and I'd managed to get out of bed...and onto my bedroom floor. It had stopped snowing, but with the snow still blocking the roads, the shop was closed. Even if the roads were clear, I might have stayed closed just so I could recover.

I was laying on my back, head toward my closet. The doors were open, so when I tilted my head back a bit, my eyes rested on The Vanishing Wall. All the details of my Grandpa Roan's disappearance.

Now that the Heart Attack case was solved my thoughts circled around my grandfather.

Who in the bloodsucking fangs was Belinda Hollow? Why had she entered Arteria Falls before my grandfather disappeared and before the notes were left?

My phone dinged, but it was just another picture in the endless parade Lacey had been sending me of her and her roommates snuggling Reginald. I smiled, glad the cat was getting some love. I crossed my fingers—metaphorically of course, my fingers were too sore to actually cross them—that he might have found a new home.

Belinda. Belinda. Belinda.

I'd tried researching her, but came up with a whole blood bag of nothing.

Many useful contacts had come into my life when I worked with my grandfather, including a couple who might be able to find Belinda for me. I'd messaged them, but it would take time.

My mind rewound to the notes left on my door. How had they gotten there? Maybe I should ask Judith, since she'd found a way around my doorbell camera too.

I sat up so fast my head started pounding out a drum beat. "Ugh, why. Stooooop."

After the room stopped spinning and the nausea subsided, I pulled myself into my wheelchair.

I found Lynnae in the kitchen making blood blends. Calder had made her swear she wouldn't try to go to work in this snow. She'd agreed very reluctantly. Her pent-up energy was apparently going into very scientific blending. She had a notebook and all kinds of instruments out.

"Josie! I need you to try blend number fifteen and compare it to blend seventeen."

"Not sixteen?" I asked.

She curled her lip. "Sixteen was a complete bust."

I laughed. "Okay, I'll be your guinea pig, but then I need a huge favor."

"Need me to rub your back? That's no problem. We can put some electrical stimulation on it first—"

"Lynnae! That's not it. I mean, if you want to rub my back later, I wouldn't say no, but that's not the favor."

"What is it?"

I made my face as serious as possible. "We're going to a very disturbing place. You'll have to brace yourself for the horrors we'll find."

"Holy varicose veins. This is so much worse than you described."

"There was no way to adequately prepare you," I told Lynnae.

She put a hand on her throat. "Dear Goddess, is that…a flamingo riding a panther?"

I followed her gaze to the front porch, which had been cleared of snow. "I wish I could say no, but it is."

Shuddering, but not from the cold, we got out of Lynnae's SUV. I'd hoped to never cross Judith and Eddie's threshold again, but needs must.

The normally ten-minute drive across town had taken almost thirty, with one moment of terror when the SUV slid into an intersection after the light turned red. Thank the stars, no one was coming.

When I'd asked Lynnae to accompany me, she'd stepped away, holding her hands up. But she'd seen the familiar gleam in my eye that told her I couldn't wait.

"We can't get her on Zoom or something?" she'd pleaded.

"She'd just hang up on us."

Knowing I was right, my roommate had grabbed her keys. "Fine."

The pathway to the door had been cleared and salted, probably by Judith instead of Eddie.

I held onto Lynnae for support as we climbed the stairs. I almost slipped once, but she caught me.

As Lynnae glared at the flamingo riding a panther, I rang the doorbell.

Judith looked surprised to see anyone, much less me, at the door.

"Josie? I didn't think anyone would be out in this snow." She took in the cut on my cheek, a motherly look crossing her face.

"It's urgent. I really need to speak with you."

She scratched her neck. "Didn't they catch the attacker, though?"

"No, *I* caught the attacker," I clarified, wanting her to understand that I was very good at what I did. "You know what this is about."

She tried to shut the door on me for the third time that week. This time, my bestie stuck her boot out to catch the door.

"Judith. I'm not messing around."

The door eased open.

Her house was as clean as ever and smelled divine. Chocolate called to me from the kitchen, but I resisted it.

We followed Judith into her living room. Or more like nightmare room. I did my best to ignore the flamingos, having had enough of them to last me a lifetime, but Lynnae gaped, not bothering to hide her shock.

I took off my coat. "Like I said, you know why I'm here."

Twisting a lock of hair, she said, "I don't know what you mean, Josie."

"Let's not play games."

She said nothing.

"Fine, I'll spell it out for you. On Friday morning, news about the attacks spread through town. When I got home that night, I found one of your hearts on my door. I'd assumed you were following blonds around town, noting their work and home locations, then returning with a heart later." I tilted forward. "But you couldn't have followed me."

Judith grabbed the stuffed flamingo that had been perched next to her. Giving it a tight squeeze, she said, "I saw you leave that morning."

I let out a dark chuckle. "Right. You heard about the attacks that morning, concluded it must be Eddie, got a bunch of hearts together, and happened to drive down my street. All before half past eight when I left to pick up a new batch of hand-braided leashes from a woman across town?"

The poor flamingo almost lost its head as she continued to squeeze. "Yes. That's what happened."

"Judith!" I said, raising my voice. "How did you know a blond person lived in my house? How did you get around my doorbell camera? It's got a pretty wide lens."

The woman started shaking her head frantically.

"Judith, I'm tired. I'm in so much pain. How. Did. You. Get. Around. My. Camera? On Friday *and in October*. It had to be you who left me the notes."

She started rocking side to side.

"Just tell me." My voice broke on the last word and tears pooled in my eyes. "Please, Judith."

A single tear descended my cheek.

"Frickin' fangs, Judith!" Lynnae thundered. "Answer her before you rip that poor flamingo's head off."

That did it. Not my emotional plea, but the danger to her flamingo. She held the bird out, checking for damage. Confirming it was okay, she set it down.

"I used a WiFi jammer."

Of course. The camera used our WiFi to upload videos. It had no local storage. Without an internet connection, it was useless. No motion would register. No videos would be recorded.

"We weren't home when you left the first note or the heart," Lynnae mused, "so we didn't know the WiFi had temporarily gone out. And the day of the party when you left the second note, we were too busy to notice."

Judith nodded. "Exactly."

I ground my teeth. "You don't strike me as the type to have illegal technology floating around, so where did you get the jammer? I'm guessing you acquired it about four months ago."

She groaned. "I only did it because I was behind on the mortgage, okay? I'd been out of work for a while—still am—when they contacted me last fall. I live off selling my handmade items, but it isn't enough."

"When *who* contacted you?" I asked, now on the edge of the couch cushion.

Judith shrugged, her eyes wide. "Honestly, Josie, I don't know. The number was private, and they used one of those things that scrambles your voice. It was so easy. I just had to use the jammer and leave a couple notes for you. The money was substantial. I couldn't say no."

So these motherfangers who'd been taunting me about my grandfather had found a desperate woman and manipulated her. I hated them even more, but I actually felt bad for Judith. She didn't mean any harm. "Eddie doesn't help with the mortgage?"

She rolled her eyes. "No. He says I'd have to pay it whether he lives here or not, so he doesn't help me."

Ugh. Did he spend all his money on bugs?

"Did you write the notes?"

"No." She patted the couch. "They taped a manila envelope to the bottom of a bench in the park. It was kind of exciting, like being in a spy movie, or..." She trailed off upon noticing the death stare I was sending her way.

"How did they pay you?"

"Cash in the envelope alongside the notes."

"Does the name Belinda Hollow ring a bell?

"No. Should it?"

I ignored her question. "Have they contacted you since October?"

Judith wrung her hands. "The day before I met you, they contacted me again. I picked up another envelope. After I met you, though, it didn't feel right. You weren't just a stranger anymore. They called me back when I didn't leave the note."

"How did they know?"

She shook her head. "They must be watching me or you...or both of us. I got another private call. Whoever was on the other end of the line was very upset. I told them I wanted to give the envelope, with all the cash, back. They made it clear that wasn't an option, so I hung up on them."

I stood up, leaning heavily on my crutch. "You still have the envelope?"

She jumped up and scurried from the room. Lynnae pulled me back down. "You need to sit, Jos."

Seconds later, Judith was back with the manila envelope. I stared at it for a second before taking it from her.

She wasn't lying about the cash. It was more than substantial. After setting it on the coffee table, I pulled out a piece of plain ivory cardstock.

Lynnae grabbed my arm as I flipped it over.

We're still waiting, Josie.

That was it? Fangs. How was I supposed to know what they wanted me to find if they didn't give me any hints?

I shoved the note in my pocket, feeling it bend. I didn't care. The note could bite me.

We left in a hurry, but before Judith closed the door, I said, "If they call back, tell them you delivered the note." She moved to close the door. "And Judith? Do you ever make anything for pets?"

"So these cameras will record even if the WiFi goes out?" my cousin asked.

"Yep. They store video locally. You'd have to try a lot harder to get around these babies." I held the shop's tablet out to him. "The app has a live video feed. You should probably get familiar with the layout in case you need to access the cameras while I'm not here."

A few hours before, the shop's new security cameras had come online. I wasn't risking my house or my business again. Between Wyatt, Judith, and whoever she worked for, I was tired of feeling vulnerable. My house had been set up the day before.

The cameras, and the rest of the security system, were expensive, but it was worth it.

"I'm so glad you got cameras for the shop too. Did you hear they found a whole crazy stalker board in Wyatt's house?" Dawk shuddered.

"I'm not surprised in the least bit. He would have needed it to keep track of all the details."

My phone rang, so I left Dawk to play with the cameras and rolled to the storeroom. It was a private number. My whole body tensed. "Hello?"

"Well done, Josie," a scrambled voice said.

"Who are you?"

"We've been a bit disappointed in you over the past few months. You haven't found what we need."

"I have no clue what—"

They cut me off. "Josie, really? You're better than that. You figured Judith out, after all. Everything you need is already in your possession."

"That isn't help—"

"We can't leave you notes anymore, what with your fancy new cameras. But we'll be in touch."

The line went dead.

I pounded my fist on a massive bag of dog food.

They knew about my cameras. They seemed to know everything…except whatever they wanted me to find.

Rubbing my eyes and getting mascara everywhere, I considered their words.

Everything you need is already in your possession.

The notes they sent? The excised fangs they'd included with the second note?

Wait. The fangs. I was an idiot. Did I not know two fantastic anatomy researchers? Why hadn't I considered the fangs before? I'd assumed they were nothing more than a scare tactic.

I dialed Lynnae. "Hey, roomie. Are you busy?"

THE END

Josie returns for more antics and investigations
in Summer 2023. In the meantime, visit
https://BookHip.com/MFMVTXH to get a **FREE**

PREQUEL NOVELLA for the Vampire Pet Boutique Mysteries. Check it out below:

Almost Fangmous

Josie Wixx, pet-boutique owner and disabled vampire, just wants to enjoy the best vampire music festival of the year, Stakestock, which is held in her gorgeous town of Arteria Falls, Colorado—a snug little community pressed against the Rocky Mountains. But before she can even dip her fangs into the music, she stumbles across one of her favorite frontmen dead on the ground.

With the whole festival at stake, Josie is asked to resurrect the investigative skills she acquired while assisting her grandfather, the town's old private investigator. With the help of a borrowed neon-orange mobility scooter, Josie zips around the festival to look for answers, using the scooter's horn on anyone who gets in her way. But the more she digs, the more Josie realizes the killer might be closer than anyone could have guessed.

Scan below to download!

For the scoop on upcoming books, insider info, and more fun content, join **Elle's Facebook reader group** at https://www.facebook.com/groups/ellewrenburke!

Thank you!

Thank you for reading *The Tell-Fang Heart*! I hope you enjoyed reading it as much as I enjoyed writing it. Can I ask you a favor? If you have a few minutes, can you leave a review on Amazon or Goodreads? I would really appreciate it.

Josie returns for more antics and investigations in Summer 2023.

Interested in a **FREE PREQUEL NOVELLA** featuring disabled sleuth Josie Wixx? Go to https://BookHip.com/MFMVTXH to download *Almost Fangmous*.

For the scoop on upcoming books, insider info, and more fun content, join **Elle's Facebook reader group** at https://www.facebook.com/groups/ellewrenburke.

Follow me on:

Instagram @ellewrenburke.author

Facebook @ellewrenburke

Twitter @ElleBurke8

About the Author

Elle Wren Burke is a paranormal cozy mystery author who writes witty, fun books with strong females as protagonists.

Elle also lives with Hypermobile Ehlers-Danlos Syndrome, a connective tissue disease. She has Master's degrees in Geography and Business. Elle lives in Arizona with her husband and fur babies. She enjoys puzzles, baking, and board games.

Learn more about Elle and stay up to date on new books at https://elleburkeauthor.com/

For the scoop on upcoming books, insider info, and more fun content, join Elle's Facebook reader group at https://www.facebook.com/groups/ellewrenburke!

Follow Elle on:

Instagram @ellewrenburke.author

Facebook @ellewrenburke

Twitter @ElleBurke8

Also By Elle Wren Burke

Vampire Pet Boutique Mysteries

Almost Fangmous (Free Prequel)

A Fang to Remember

The Tell-Fang Heart

Prickly Pear Psychic Mysteries

Mediums & Murder

Tea & Talismans

Canines & Cacti

Mascara & Mayhem

Made in the USA
Monee, IL
30 June 2023

38209131R10148